Apache

by Alan Wilson
with Rita Vigil Martine

An Audio-Cassette Program

Especially created to accompany this
book are 4 instructional audio cassettes.
They are available from the publisher.

AUDIO·FORUM

A Division of Jeffrey Norton Publishers
Guilford, Connecticut

Copyright ◀ ◀ ◀ ◀

Apache (Jicarilla)

ISBN 0-88432-903-8   text and cassettes
ISBN 0-88432-905-4   text only

Published by Audio-Forum,
a division of Jeffrey Norton Publishers, Inc., On-the-Green, Guilford, CT 06437-2635

Cover design: Apache horsemen of an early period as interpreted by the artist.

Dedication ◄ ◄ ◄ ◄

Díí naałtsoozii éí Abáachii má, shį́į́ nahii'iłchín shį́į́ natsóóyį́í má, naláach'į'yé hiikai'íí, nakéék'eyé shį́į́ nazaa'íí ádaat'éo.

This work is dedicated to the Jicarilla Apache and to their children and grandchildren, who represent the future of their culture and their language.

Nii' nahii'máá át'é, yá nahiika'éé át'é.
The earth is our mother, the sky is our father.
    — *Jicarilla Apache belief*

Ík'ą́ą́'yé íídéńká áshį́í nádńdááł. Éí nantwogo ániilé, shiiyii'į́í.
Run to the mountain and back. It will make you strong, My Son.
    — *Jicarilla Apache exhortation to a young warrior*

Sádńleeł dá'yá'déé nzhǫ́.
Long life, old age, everything good.
    — *Jicarilla Apache ceremonial saying for protection*

Acknowledgments ◀ ◀ ◀ ◀

Special acknowledgment must be given to the Jicarilla Apache Tribal Council, whose encouragement and support provided impetus for the undertaking of this work. I am also grateful to Ardela Veneno and to the many other Jicarilla Apaches, including those working in the Jicarilla Apache Culture Center, in Dulce, New Mexico, who have provided information before and throughout the writing of the book and who choose to remain anonymous. I wish as well to thank Ellyn Lathan of the Mescalero Apache Culture Center in Mescalero, New Mexico, and Edgar Perry, Director of the White Mountain Apache Culture Center in Fort Apache, Arizona, for the amiable and valuable conversations I had with them about their languages and for furnishing pertinent written and recorded materials. As for my earlier work with Mescalero Apache, I wish to express my gratitude to Gerald Comanche for his help with the language and for the tape recordings we made together.

In addition, I am especially indebted to Susan McGoldrick for her cheerful and highly competent approach to the difficult work of placing the myriad diacritical marks throughout the entire text, and to Craig Spooner, Department Chair of Electronic Publishing Technology at the University of New Mexico–Gallup Campus, for his invaluable expertise in, and his enthusiasm for, the critical task of formatting the book. I also heartily thank Chuck Simms, sound-engineering expert in Tucson, for the outstanding job of preparing the tape recordings for publication. And, finally, I want to acknowledge my gratitude to Suzanne Hoffmann for her successful efforts in contributory research, and to Kaye Wilson and John Riley for their time spent as subjects for the field testing of the course, for their proofreading skills, and for their wise and useful suggestions along the way.

Alan Wilson
Gallup, New Mexico
1996

Contents ◀◀◀◀

Introduction ◀◀◀◀

This basic course in the Jicarilla Apache language provides the foundation for mastering the essential vocabulary and sentence structures used in everyday Apache conversation.

A pronunciation guide precedes the lesson units and presents all of the sounds of the language in a format designed to facilitate learning.* The Guide provides technical as well as simplified explanations of how Jicarilla sounds are formed. Careful reading by the learner of these definitions, in conjunction with use of the recording, will ensure accurate pronunciation of the sounds. The recordings of the pronunciation guide and, indeed, all of the recordings of the course have been made by a native speaker of Jicarilla Apache, Rita Vigil Martine.

Following the pronunciation guide, the first lesson unit introduces useful phrases and questions which are reintroduced in later units. Memorization of this material will establish language patterns that may be used to create new and original combinations. Lesson units 2–21 include dialogs, vocabulary, grammatical explanations relating to the dialogs, reviews, new vocabulary practice, and comprehension exercises. Cultural notes about Jicarilla Apache folkways, taboos, and idiomatic usages may be found in the lesson units and, especially, in the appendix section of supplementary materials following lesson unit 21. Selective comparisons of terms in Jicarilla Apache, Mescalero Apache, Western Apache and Navajo are also made.

A discussion of several notable syntactical differences between Jicarilla Apache and English may be found in Appendix 4, "Notes on Some Linguistic Aspects of Jicarilla Apache."

Here are a few basic differences in grammatical structures between the two languages:

1. The verb comes at the end of the sentence.

2. Adjectives regularly follow nouns.

3. In spoken Jicarilla Apache the subject and possessive pronouns are, in most cases, differentiated by tone (shíí — I, shii — my). In written form, possessive pronouns are prefixed to the noun (shiika'éé — my father).

* The writing system or orthography used is one developed by Robert Young and William Morgan for the Navajo language and and later employed for work in both Mescalero and Western Apache.

4. Prepositions denoting position, direction, or other characteristics are represented by a syllable (called *enclitic*) which always follows a word or name and, in writing, is attached to it (Santa Fe'yé — *to Santa Fe, at Santa Fe*). These enclitics are pronounced as part of the preceding word, be it a noun, verb, or other form.

5. Enclitics are also used to particularize verbs and nouns (na'iizii — *he works,* na'iizii'íí — *he particularly works, his work;* nahiikéyaa — *our land,* nahiikéyaa'íí — *our particular land).*

Notwithstanding these intriguing grammatical differences between Jicarilla Apache and English, the learner who is willing to keep working with the course materials until mastered will be able to make significant and rewarding progress toward fluent speech in one of the most fascinating native languages in North America.

A Guide to Jicarilla Apache Pronunciation

Short Vowel Sounds

There are four basic short vowel sounds in Jicarilla Apache. These sounds are represented by a single vowel letter:

a	áń *(he, she)*	gah *(rabbit)*	Like *a* in *father*
e	dzé *(berry)*	é *(clothes)*	Like *e* in *met*
i	sis *(belt)*	chish *(wood, tree)*	Like *i* in *fit*
o	gó *(also)*	kóh *(water)*	Like *o* in *hope*

Long Vowel Sounds

Each of the above short vowel sounds may be lengthened or held for a slightly longer duration. The lengthened sounds are represented by doubled vowel letters:

aa	saa *(language, word)*	cháá *(beaver)*
ee	mee *(with him, her, it)*	hooyéé *(nice, beautiful)*
ii	shíí *(I, me)*	shiibii *(my stomach)*
oo	doo *(not)*	bóó *(cow)*

Tone

Jicarilla Apache vowel sounds are either high or low in tone. For example, all of the Jicarilla words above with accent marks are higher in tone than those without. Tone may affect meaning:

na'iizii *(he, she works)*   na'íízii *(you work)*
gáh *(juniper)*   gah *(rabbit)*

Off-Glide and On-Glide

Jicarilla vowel sounds may glide in pitch. The off-glide is indicated with an accent mark over the initial vowel letter, the on-glide with a mark over the second vowel letter:

gahée *(coffee)*   haéé'ą *(all right)*

Nasalization

Jicarilla Apache vowel sounds may be nasalized. Such vowels are pronounced through the nasal passage. Nasalization is indicated with a hook (reverse *cedilla*) subscripted to the vowel letter:

sǫǫs *(star, wart)*   kįį *(store, building, town)*

Nasalization of vowels may affect meaning:

shíí *(I, me)*   shį́į́ *(and)*

Dipthongs

ai   hai *(winter);* kái'ii *(three)* Somewhat like the *y* in *my*, but pronounced tersely and without off-glide.

ao   ao, aoo *(yes)* No real English equivalent.

ei   séí *(sand)* Somewhat like *ay* in *bay*, pronounced tersely.

oi   ndói *(mountain lion)* Somewhat like *ew* in *chewy*, spoken tersely and without off-glide.

Consonants

'   shá'ii'áí *(west)* The apostrophe (') represents a glottal stop, the interval sound commonly heard in the English expression *oh-oh!*

b   báala *(shovel)* A voiceless and unaspirated bilabial stop, something like *p* in *spoke*.

ch' ch'ał *(hat)* Glottal closure and release from approximate English *ch* tongue position.

d   dooda *(no)* A voiceless, unaspirated alveolar stop, something like *t* in *store*.

dl   dlǫ́' *(prairie dog)* Like *dl* in *muddling*, without the *schwa* between the *d* and *l* sounds.

dz   dzé *(berry)* Like *dz* in *adze*.

g   góyą́ *(intelligent)* A voiceless, unaspirated back palatal stop, something like *k* in *skid*.

gh   shiigha̦ *(my home)* A voiced velar spirant, with no English equivalent. The tongue is in position to say *get*, but a slight opening between back of tongue and palate allows air to come through with voice.

h   (syllable initial) ha'go *(when)* A voiceless glottal spirant, somewhat like *h* in *hay*.

h   (syllable final) kóh *(water)* A voiceless glottal spirant, as above.

hw   hwiigo *(quickly)* Like *wh* in *where*.

j   jee *(pitch, gum)* A voiceless unaspirated apico-alveolar affricate, much like the *j* in *jig*, but with the tongue in the *d* position.

k   kéyaa *(land, reservation)* An aspirated back palatal stop, somewhat like *k* in English *kin*.

kw   kwéé *(here)* Like *qu* in *quill*.

k'   k'os *(clouds)* A glottalized palato-velar stop, made from the *k* position by releasing the tongue from the palatal area with a simultaneous release of the glottis.

l   lázis *(glove)* A voiced lateral, like *ll* in *mellow*.

ł   łe' *(some)* A voiceless lateral, produced with the tongue in the *l* position and aspirating laterally (along the side or sides of the tongue) without voicing.

t   ntǫ́ǫ́'é *(bad, ugly)* This sound is aspirated. Contrast English *toe* with the Jicarilla Apache word given here. Notice that the Apache word is pronounced with both aspiration and labialization.

t'   t'á *(feather)* A glottalized alveolo-palatal stop. The tongue in the *t* position with tip against the alveolar ridge and the glottis are simultaneously released.

tł   tłah *(ointment)* A voiceless, laterally-aspirated alveolo-palatal affricate. The sound is produced from the *dl* or *tl* position with lateral aspiration. See *ł* above.

tł' tł'oh *(grass)* A glottalized *tł,* with simultaneous release of tongue and closed glottis. Compare with *tłah* in the previous example.

ts tsé *(rock)* An aspirated alveolo-palatal affricate, like *ts* in *bets,* but more strongly aspirated.

ts' ts'e *(sagebrush)* A glottalized alveolo-palatal affricate. This voiceless, glottalized *ts* is produced through simultaneous release of the tongue and closed glottis. Compare with *tsé* directly above.

zh zháał *(money)* A voiced alveolo-palatal spirant, somewhat like *z* in *azure.*

The consonant sounds represented by *ch, m, n*, s, sh, w, y,* and *z* are very similar in pronunciation to their English equivalents.

*n nshdázha *(your younger sister)* An apico-alveolar resonant, like *n* in *nice.* This sound functions widely in Jicarilla Apache as a complete syllable, known as syllabic *n* and may, in slow, deliberate speech, be pronounced as *ni-.* It may be low in tone as in *nbíilii* (your car) or high-toned as in *ńla* (your hand). Two syllabic *n*'s may occur together, e.g., *ńnyá* (you arrived).

Note: the length of the vowel sound of a word may not be the same in isolation as it is in a contextual pattern, or it may vary from speaker to speaker and from situation to situation. For example, the question indicator *he,* pronounced with a short vowel sound in interrogative context, sounds longer, more like *hee,* when pronounced in isolation, as in a vocabulary listing, or in hesitation while prefacing a spoken question. Similarly, tone in a word used contextually may vary from that used in the same word in isolation. A case in point is the word *iyáná'* (what), which in a contextual configuration such as *Iyáná' hánt'íí?* (What do you want?), is usually pronounced with both final vowel sounds high in tone, as marked above. In a vocabulary list the same word may be pronounced with the final vowel sound low in tone, i.e., *iyána'.* Most of the words in this book appear in contextual situations with far higher frequency than they do in isolation. Therefore, for the sake of consistency, vowel length and vowel tone representations and markings in this work reflect contextual rather than lexical frequency.

Unit 1 ◀◀◀◀

Introductory questions and useful phrases

Dá nzhǫ́. — It is good. Jicarilla greeting.
Aoo, dá nzhǫ́. — Yes, it is good.

Ha'ą́ńsį? — How are you?
Doo ánsį. — I am fine.

He Abáachii miizaa diints'e? — Do you understand the Apache language?
Áłts'íísdéo diists'e. — I understand a little.

Ha'shį́į́ nandá? — Where are you from?
Lósiishį́į́ naashá. — I am from Dulce.

Ha'yé dínyá? — Where are you going?
Shiighą'yé déyá. — I am going home (to my home).

Ha'go dá'kwéé dínyá? — When are you going there?
Yiską́o dá'kwéé déyá. — I am going there tomorrow.

He ą́'ee goosk'as? — Is it cold there?
Aoo, haigo ą́'ee goosk'as. — Yes, it's cold there in the winter.

He ą́'ee nił gooyéé? — Do you like it there?
Aoo, ą́'ee dá shił gooyéé. — Yes, I really like it there.

Abáachii méoniisįį hásht'į́į́. — I want to learn Apache.
Nch'ooshdé. — I'll help you.

Ihéedń. — Thank you.
Haéé'ą. — Response to *ihéedń*. This term is also used in parting.

Nzhǫ́go nandá. — Be careful.
Nzhǫ́go na'íílo. — Drive carefully.
Nádńdááł — Come back.

1

Vocabulary

1. dá — quite, just
2. nzhǫ́ — it is good
3. aoo — yes
4. ha'áńńsį? — how are you?
5. doo ánsį. — I am fine.
6. he — a question indicator
7. Abáachii — Apache (Jicarilla Apache only)
8. miizaa — his, her, their language
9. diints'e — you understand it
10. áłts'íísdéo — a little, a bit
11. ha' — where
12. shį́į́ — from
13. nandá — you walk about
14. Lósii — Dulce, New Mexico
15. Losiishį́į́ — from Dulce
16. naashá — I walk about
17. ha'yé — where to (also at where)
18. dínyá — you (singular) are going
19. shiighą — my home
20. shiighą'yé — to my home
21. déyá — I am going
22. nghą — your (singular) home
23. Lósii'yé — at Dulce
24. ha'go — when
25. dá'kwéé — there (toward there)
26. yiską́o — tomorrow
27. he — question indicator
28. á'ee — there (at there)
29. goosk'as — cold (atmosphere only)
30. hai — winter
31. haigo — in the winter (literally *winter when*)
32. nił — with you
33. gooyéé — it is nice, beautiful, good
34. nił gooyéé — you like it (with you it is good)
35. shił — with me
36. dá shił gooyéé — I really like it
37. méoniisįį — I learn it, am learning it
38. hásht'į́į́ — I want, wish
39. nzhǫ́go — nicely, carefully
40. na'íílo — you drive

Cultural note

A typical Jicarilla greeting format consists of the expression *dá nzhǫ́*, given above, and a brief, gentle contact of the palms of the right hand. The touch is very light, with no squeezing, macho crunching, or hydraulic pumping of the arms as is sometimes the way of *Mągdanii*, the White Man. In parting one usually says *haéé'ą* (all right), also pronounced *haíí'ą*. This word is also widely used to express agreement. Another parting term is *hahíínde*, somewhat equivalent to English *goodbye*.

2

Unit 2 ◀ ◀ ◀ ◀

Dialog

Dá nzhǫ́. — Greetings (it is good).
Aoo, dá nzhǫ́. — Yes, greetings.

Ha' án̄sį? — How are you?
Doo ánsį. — I am fine.

He Abáachii miizaa diints'e? — Do you understand the Apache language?
Dooda, Abáachii doo diists'e da — No, I don't understand Apache.

He díí méoǹsįį? — Are you learning it?
Aoo, méoniisįį — Yes, I am learning it.

He dá nił hooyéé? — Do you like it?
Aoo, dá shił hooyéé. — Yes, I like it.

He díí ch'éh ánł'įį́? — Is it difficult for you?
Dooda, doo ch'éh ásh'įį́ da. — No, it is not difficult for me.

Ha'yéną́ą isgwéela nándééh? — Where do you go to school?
Lósii'yé isgwéela náshdééh. — I go to school in Dulce.

Nshdázha iyáná' yéoniisįį? — What is your younger brother learning?
Abáachii yéoniisįį — He is learning Apache.

He áń Lósii'yé isgwéela nádééh? — Does he go to school in Dulce?
Dooda, Chama'yé isgwéela nádééh. — No, he goes to school in Chama.

Vocabulary

1. aoo — yes
2. he — question indicator always preceding question phrase
3. Abáachii miizaa — the Apache language
4. diints'e — you understand it, hear it

3

5. diists'e — I understand, hear it
6. dooda — no
7. doo diists'e da — I don't understand it
8. díí — this, it (a referent in this case to *Abáachii*)
9. méońsįį — you are learning it
10. méoniisįį — I am learning it
11. dá — a particle used as a filler and sometimes as an intensifier
12. nił — with you
13. hooyéé — it is good, nice
14. nił (nł) hooyéé — you like it
15. shił hooyéé — I like it
16. ch'éh ánł'íí — it is difficult for you
17. ch'éh ásh'íí — it is difficult for me
18. ha' — where
19. yé — in this case, *at*
20. ną́ą — a filler suffix with no separate meaning
21. ha'yéną́ą — at where
22. isgwéela — school, from Spanish *escuela*
23. nándééh — you attend
24. Lósii — Dulce, New Mexico
25. náshdééh — I attend
26. nshdázha — your younger brother or sister
27. iyáná' — what
28. yéoniisįį — he, she is learning it
29. áń — he, she
30. Chama — a town in northern New Mexico, near Dulce
31. nádééh — he, she attends

Explanations

1. In the expression *dá nzhǫ́*, the particle *dá* is a filler and/or intensifier which can carry the meaning *just* or *quite*. *Nzhǫ́* is widely used to mean *it is good, beautiful, nice, harmonious.*

2. *Ha'áńńsį* is used to ask about one's general state or condition. The element *ha'* has several meanings, here conveying the query *how, in what way*. *Áńńsį*, a second person verb carries the sense of wanting or having an appetite for. It may be compared to Navajo *anínísin*, which has the same meaning. Thus, a somewhat literal connotation of the question is derived: *In what way might you be wanting?* The conventional answer *doo ánsį*, with the negative *doo*, means literally *I do not want, I have no appetite*. Again, compare Navajo *doo unisin da*. The question might also be formed as *hat'é áńńsį* or *hat'éną́ą áńńsį*, with the identical meaning.

3. The question indicator *he* must be used before a phrase to form a question. Compare Jicarilla *he* with Mescalero Apache *ha*, Western Apache *ya'*, and Navajo *da'* as common devices to indicate interrogative sentences.

4. The verb *diists'e* carries the meaning *I hear*, with inference that I therefore *understand*.

5. *Abáachii miizaa* (the Apache language) means literally *Jicarilla Apache his, her, their language*. The word *Abáachii* is commonly used to signify the Jicarilla Apache language as well as a Jicarilla Apache person or the Jicarilla Apache people, just as *Mǫgáanii* means both *White Man* and *English language*.

6. Negative expressions are formed by separating the word *dooda* into the segments *doo* and *da*. These segments then parenthesize the word or words to be made negative. Thus, *diists'e* (I understand) becomes *doo diists'e da* (I don't understand). In everyday discourse the element *da* is often not used. Examples are *doo mégosį* (I don't know) and *doo diits'e* (he, she is mischievous, literally *he, she does not hear*).

7. The verb *méoniisįį* (I am learning it) is related to Navajo *bééhooniisįįh* (I am becoming acquainted with it). Note that the 2nd person *méońsįį* (you are learning it) carries a high-toned syllabic *ń* which is paralleled by Navajo high-toned *ní* in 2nd person *bééhooníisįįh*. The common Navajo term for *I am learning it* is *bóhoosh'aah*, interestingly close to Mescalero Apache *bégush'ą'* and Western Apache *bígosh'ąął*.

8. *Nił* (with you) is shortened to *nł, ni-* becoming syllabic.

9. The term *dá shił hooyéé* may be analyzed as follows: the particle *dá*, as pointed out in number1 above, is a filler or an intensifier extensively used in Jicarilla Apache speech. A single meaning for the particle is elusive, but it sometimes conveys the meaning *just, quite*. It might be loosely compared to Navajo *t'áá*. *Dá shił hooyéé* has the verbatim meaning *quite with me it is good, pleasant, nice*. This term may be used without the particle *dá* with no change in meaning, but as such may convey slightly less intensity.

10. In Unit 1 you saw the expression *dá shił gooyéé*, in reference to Dulce, New Mexico. *Gooyéé* appears to be used primarily to express liking for a place, and *hooyéé* for the appreciation of objects, subject matter and people.

11. The expression *ch'éh ánł'íí* literally translates as *in vain you do it*, where *ch'éh* signifies *barely, unsuccesfully, in vain*, and *ánł'íí* means *you habitually do* or *make*. However, the idiom does imply difficulty rather than total impossibility.

12. *Ha'yénǫ́ǫ* may mean either *to where* or *at where*. The word is constituted of *ha'* (where), an element which cannot stand alone, *-yé*, an enclitic, or suffix meaning either *to* or *at*, depending on context, and the additional element *-nǫ́ǫ*, extensively appended as a filler to Jicarilla words and having no independent meaning. The question can as well be formulated as *Ha'yé isgwéela nándééh?* (unaccompanied by *-nǫ́ǫ*), with no change in meaning.

13. The term *isgwéela náshdééh* carries the literal meaning *school I attend*. The word *isgwéela* is from Spanish *escuela*.

14. The place name *Lósii* (Dulce, New Mexico), an Apache approximation of the borrowed Spanish word *dulce* (sweet or candy), also means *candy* in Jicarilla Apache.

15. *Nshdázha* means both *your younger brother* or *your younger sister*. Conversational context determines which one is referred to.

16. The question word *iyáná'* (what) is often shortened to *yáná'* in everyday discourse.

Review and practice with new vocabulary

1. He Mągáanii diints'e? — Do you understand English?
   Dooda, Mągáanii doo diists'e da — No, I don't understand English.

2. He Inłt'ánéé yidiits'e? — Does he, she understand Navajo?
   Aoo, Inłt'ánéé yidiits'e — Yes, he, she understands Navajo.

3. He Dawoséeo miizaa diints'e? — Do you understand Taos?
   Dawoséeo shíí Yóda diists'e. — I understand Taos and Ute.

4. Ha'yénąą méosíńsįį? — Where did you learn it?
   Koghą'yé méosésįį. — I learned it at home.
   Koghą'yé yégósįį. — He, she learned it at home.

5. Iyáná' méońsįį? — What are you learning?
   Abáachii miizaa méoniisįį — I am learning the Apache language.
   Mągáanii miizaa yéoniisįį — He is learning the English language.

6. He dá mił hooyéé? — Does he like it?
   Aoo, dá mił hooyéé. — Yes, he likes it.

7. He ch'éh áyiił'íí? — Is it difficult for him?
   Aoo, ch'éh áyiił'íí? — Yes, it is difficult for him.

8. He dá nł hooyéé? — Do you like it?
   Aoo, dá shił hooyéé. — Yes, I like it.

9. He Nadaíin méońsįį? — Are you learning Mescalero Apache?
   Łeeshchíí méoniisįį. — I am learning San Carlos Apache.

10. Iyáná' hánt'íí? — What do you want?
    Iibe' łe' hásht'íí. — I want some milk.
    Itsįį shíí mansáana hásht'íí. — I want meat and apples.

11. Iyáná' yííkát'íí? — What does he want?
    Iizee łe' yííkát'íí. — He wants some medicine.

12. He asóokala łe' hánt'íí? — Do you want some sugar?
    Kółbáíí łe' hásht'íí. — I want some tiswin. (see Cultural Note).
    Neest'áan łe' hásht'íí. — I want some vegetables.

Comprehension practice

Shíí John shíízhii.* Lósii'yé isgwéela náshdééh. Abáachii méoniisįį. Dá shił hooyéé, énda** ch'éh ásh'íí. Shiishdázha Lósii'yé doo isgwéela nádééh da. Chama'yé isgwéela nádééh. Mągáanii miizaa yéoniisįį. Dá mił hooyéé. Doo ch'éh áyiił'íí da.

   * My name is John (literally, *I John my name*).
  ** but

Questions

1. Hat'éo míízhii? — What is his name? (How his name?)
2. Ha'yénąą isgwéela nádééh? — Where does he attend school?
3. Iyáná' yéoniisįį? — What is he learning?
4. He dá mił hooyéé? — Does he like it?
5. He ch'éh áyiił'íí? — Is it difficult for him?
6. He miishdázha Lósii'yé isgwéela nádééh? — Does his brother go to school in Dulce?
7. Miishdázha ha'yé isgwéela nádééh? — Where does his brother go to school?
8. Miishdázha iyáná' yéoniisįį? — What is his brother learning?

Notice that in the beginning sentence of the Comprehension above, the first word *shíí* is an independent personal pronoun meaning *I*. Independent personal pronouns are not as widely used in Jicarilla Apache as they are in English because the subject markers are included in the verb complex. These pronouns usually serve as mild emphasis. Gender is

7

not distinguished in the third person pronoun or in the verb forms, context determining whether *he, she, it,* or *they* is meant. The independent personal pronouns are as follows:

Singular	Dual	Distributive Plural
shíí — I	nahíí — we (two)	danahíí — we (more than two)
díí — you	nahíí — you (two)	danahíí — you (more than two)
bíí, áń — he, she, it	bíí — they (two)	daabíí — they (more than two)

Cultural Note

The Jicarilla Apaches and other Apachean speakers have traditionally made a beverage known as tiswin. Corn is put into a container of water or buried in the ground until it begins to sprout. It is then ground into a meal and put into water with various herbs and boiled for four or five days. When the mixture is cooled the sediment of corn and herbs settles to the bottom and the fermented grayish liquid at the top is drawn off for drinking. The native terms for this drink are: Jicarilla, *kółbáíí;* Mescalero, *túłbááí;* and Navajo, *tó łibáhí,* all translated as *gray water* (literally *water gray*).

A selective comparison of Apachean terms

I want fish; I want corn; she wants water.

Jicarilla:	Łógee hásht'íí.
	Naadą' hásht'íí.
	Kóh yííkát'íí.

Mescalero:	Łuuye hásht'íí.
	Inaadą' hásht'íí.
	Tú yííkát'íí.

Western:	Łóg hásht'íí.
	Nadą' hásht'íí.
	Tú hát'íí.

Navajo:	Łóó' nisin.
	Naadą́ą́' nisin.
	Tó yinízin.

Unit 3 ◄◄◄◄

Dialog

Ha'yénáą́ dínyá? — Where are you going?
Shiigha'yé déyá. — I am going home (to my home).
Kịị'yé déyá. — I am going to town.

Ha'go dínyá? — When are you going?
Yiskáọo déyá. — I am going tomorrow.
Dákoo déyá. — I am going now.
Lasóongo déyá. — I am going on Saturday.

He nbíilii góníí? — Do you have a car?
Aoo, shiibíilii góníí. — Yes, I have a car.

He nbíilii na'iizii? — Does your car work?
Aoo, na'iizii, énda bííł miikoo łe' hásht'íí́. — Yes, it works but I want some gasoline.

Ha'yé nghą? — Where do you live? (Where is your home?)
Ndé'ee shiighą. Doo aada da. — My home is over there. It is not far.

Haéé'ą — Goodbye.
Aoo, haéé'ą — Yes, goodbye.

Vocabulary

1. ha'yénáą́ — where to (also *at where*)
2. dínyá — you are going
3. shiighą — my home
4. shiighą'yé — to my home
5. déyá — I go, am going
6. kịị — town, store, building
7. kịị'yé — to town, to the store
8. ha'go — when?
9. yiskáọ — tomorrow
10. dákoo — now
11. Lasóongo — on Saturday
12. he — question indicator
13. bííł — car
14. nbíilii — your car
15. góníí — it exists
16. aoo — yes
17. shiibíilii — my car
18. na'iizii — he, she, it works

9

19. énda — but
20. bííł miikoo — gasoline (car water; note possessed form of *kóh* (water) is *-koo*)
21. łe' — some
22. hásht'íí — I want
23. nghą — your home
24. ndé'ee — there, over there
25. doo aada da — it is not far

Explanations

1. As noted in Unit 2, *ha'*, a word of several meanings, signifies *where* at the beginning of the above dialog. The enclitic (a segment suffixed to a preceding word and dependent upon it for meaning) *-yé* connotes *toward, to,* or *at*. When used together the two elements are separated by a glottal stop, represented by ('). Words ending in an unglottalized vowel, such as *shiigha* (my home), also take a glottal stop when a vowel or semi-vowel-initial enclitic is suffixed: *shiigha'yé* (to my home, at my home). You will also hear *shiigha'ee* (at my home).

2. *Dínyá* is a second person verb form meaning *you are going, you go*. The letter *n* in this word represents a syllabic low-toned *n* sound, i.e., it represents a syllable whose full form is *-ni-*. Thus, the tonal pattern of *dínyá* is high-low-high (dí-n-yá). The native speaker in the cassette recording makes clear the tonal motif of this word. A high-toned syllabic *n* is marked with an *accent aigu*: *ń*, as in *méońsįį* (you are learning it). See the final paragraph in *A Guide to Jicarilla Apache Pronunciation* at the beginning of this book.

3. The word *shiigha* is made up of the singular possessive pronoun *shii-* (my) and the noun *gha* (home, dwelling place).

4. *Kįį* can mean *town(s), store(s), house(s), building(s)*. A town is a place where there are buildings, therefore *kįį* may carry the collective meaning *town*. Compare Mescalero *kį*, Western Apache *kįh*, and Navajo *kin*. Note that there are very few plural forms for Jicarilla Apache nouns. Thus *kįį* means *town or towns, store or stores*, and so on.

5. *Déyá* is a first person verb meaning *I start to go, I go, am going*.

6. Note that the word order in the sentence pattern is possessed object (shiigha), preposition (yé), verb (déyá). Thus, a literal translation of *shiigha'yé déyá* is *my home to I am going*.

7. The word *ha'go* means *when* if used to ask a question about the future. It carries the filler suffix *-nąą* in the above dialog, but may be used without it.

10

8. *Lasóon* (Saturday) is a Jicarilla approximation of English *ration*, in reference to the provisions dealt out on Saturdays to the tribe by the federal government in the earlier 1800s and later, after the establishment of a reservation at Dulce, New Mexico in 1887.

9. The question indicator *he* functions somewhat like English *do, does.*

10. The unpossessed form for the word *car* is *bíít,* apparently borrowed from the last syllable of English *automo-bile. Nbíilii* (your car(s)) is made up of the singular possessive pronoun syllabic *n* (your) and the possessed form of *bíít.* The singular third person possessive pronoun is *mii-*, thus, *miibíilii,* his car, her car. The possessive pronouns (my, your, his, her, et al.) are, as you have seen, prefixed to nouns in Jicarilla Apache. The possessive pronouns are:

Singular	**Dual**	**Distributive Plural**
shii — my	nahii — our (two)	danahii — our (more than two)
n — your (syllabic n)	nahii — your (two)	danahii — your (more than two)
mii — his, her, its	mii — their (two)	daamii — their (more than two)

Examples:

Singular
shiichóó — my grandmother
nchóó — your grandmother
miichóó — his, her grandmother

Dual
nahiichóó — our grandmother
nahiichóó — your grandmother
miichóó — their grandmother

Distributive Plural
danahiichóó — our grandmothers (more than two)
danahiichóó — your grandmothers (more than two)
damiichóó — their grandmothers (more than two)

11. The word *góníí* means *it exists.* Therefore, the phrase *shiibíilii góníí* is rendered literally as *my car it exists,* i.e., *I have a car.* The opposite of *góníí* is *édįį* (it does not exist, he or she is deceased), thus *shiibíilii édįį* is translated as *I do not have a car.*

12. Ndé'ee and ą́'ee both mean *there, over there,* in terms of location rather than direction toward. Another word for locational *there* is ą́ch'į.

Review and practice with new vocabulary

1. Shiigha'yé déyá. — I am going home.
   Dziłyé deeyá (or *deesyá*). — He, she is going to the mountains.
   Kįį'yé déyá. — I am going to the store.

2. He nghą'yé dínyá? — Are you going to your home?
   He kósiłką'yé deeyá? — Is he going to the lake?
   He kóńlįį'yéyé dínyá? — Are you going to the river?

3. Shiizháalii góníí — I have money
   Miilįį' góníí — He, she has a horse, horses, livestock
   He nmósha góníí? — Do you have a cat?

4. Shii'iibe' édįį — I don't have milk
   Miimansáana édįį — He, she doesn't have an apple, apples
   Shiichíníí édįį — I don't have a dog, dogs

5. Shiigha'yé na'iisii — I work at my home
   Miigha'yé na'iizii — He, she works at his, her home

6. Doo na'iisii da — I don't work
   Doo na'iizii da — He, she doesn't work
   Bííł doo na'iizii da — The car doesn't work.

7. Adą́dą́ na'sézii. — I worked yesterday.
   He adą́dą́ na'síńzii? — Did you work yesterday?
   Adą́dą́ miigha'yé na'iiszii. — He worked at his home yesterday.

8. Mansáana łe' hásht'įį. — I want some apples.
   Íshǫǫsh łe' yííkát'įį. — She, he wants some salt.

9. Łeet'áan doo hásht'įį da. — I don't want bread
   Kóh doo yííkát'įį da. — He, she doesn't want water

10. Iyáná' ágólé? — What are you going to make?
    Ísee ágoshłé. — I am going to make a pot.
    Ísee ágolé. — She is going to make a pot.

11. He ísee goshtł'ish ágonlaa? — Did you make a clay pot?
    Ísee goshtł'ish doo ágoshłaa da. — I didn't make a clay pot.
    Bíí ísee goshtł'ish ágolaa. — She made a clay pot.

12. Iyáná' ánlé? — What are you making?
    Káził áshłé. — I am making stew.
    Káził áyiilé. — She is making stew.

13. Íseezis hishtł'ół. — I am weaving a basket.
    He íseezis hintł'ół? — Are you weaving a basket?
    Bíí íseezis yitł'ół. — She is weaving a basket.

14. Íseezis sétł'ół. — I wove a basket.
    He íseezis síntł'ół? — Did you weave a basket?
    Íseezis yistł'ół. — She wove a basket.

Comprehension Practice

Shíí Joe shíízhii. Yiskąo shiighą'yé déyá. Shiighą'yé na'iisii. Ndé'ee shiighą. Doo aada
da. Shiibíilii góníí. Shiibíilii na'iizii, énda bííł miikoo hásht'íí.

Questions

1. Hat'éo míízhii? — What is his name?
2. Ha'yénąą deeyá? — Where is he going?
3. Ha'yé na'iizii? — Where does he work.
4. Ha'yénąą miighą? — Where is his home?
5. He miibíilii góníí? — Does he have a car?
6. He miibíilii na'iizii? — Does his car work?
7. Iyáná' yííkát'íí? — What does he want?

Cultural Note

The Jicarilla Apaches are among the speakers of Southern Athabascan languages or
dialects. The Apachean languages are a sub-group of this larger family. The members
of this linguistic stock include Jicarilla, Mescalero, Chiricahua, Lipan, Kiowa-Apache,
Western Apache and Navajo. Western Apache embraces five mutually intelligible
dialects: San Carlos, Cibecue, White Mountain, and Northern and Southern Tonto.
Navajo comprises the largest single tribe of Southern Athabascan speakers. The term
Jicarilla is derived from Spanish *jicara*, a term for a cup, gourd, or small basket. The
name was applied to the Jicarilla Apaches who were early known, and are to this day,
for their artistry in weaving fine basketry from willow (*k'ai'*) and sumac (*k'ii*).

A selective comparison of some Apachean terms

Where are you going? I am going to my home.

Jicarilla:	Ha'yé dínyá? Shiighą'yé déyá.
Mescalero:	Ha'yá dínya? Shiku'wą'yá dé'ya.
Western:	Hayú dínyaa? Shigowąyú díyáá.
Navajo:	Háágóó díníyá? Shighangóó déyá.

Unit 4 ◀◀◀◀

Dialog

Iyáná' ánł'íí? — What are you doing?
Doo yá'ásh'íí da dákoo. — I'm not doing anything now.

He na'íízii'yé dínyá? — Are you going to work?
Aoo, dák'adéé — Yes, soon.

Ha'náą na'íízii? — Where do you work?
Isgwéela'yé na'iisii — I work at a school.
Koghą'yé na'iisii — I work at home.

Ńną'áá ha'yénąą na'iizii? Where does your older brother work?
Shííną'áá háasbila'yé na'iizii. My older brother works at the (a) hospital.

Jim míízhii ya? — His name is Jim, isn't it?
Dooda, Joe míízhii. — No, his name is Joe.

Vocabulary

1. iyáná' — what
2. ánł'íí — you are doing
3. doo yá'ásh'íí da — I am not doing anything
4. dákoo — now
5. na'íízii — you work
6. dínyá — you go, are going
7. dák'adéé — soon
8. ha'náą — where
9. isgwéela — school
10. koghą — home
11. na'iisii — I work
12. ną'áá — older brother
13. ńną'áá — your older brother
14. míízhii — his, her name
15. ya — isn't it?

Explanations

1. The interrogative word *iyáná'* is generally used to preface a *what* question. The term *yáh?* (what?) is employed as a reaction to a statement not understood well or poorly heard.

2. *Ánł'íí* means *you habitually do or make.* Remember that the apostrophe (') represents a glottal stop. Listen carefully to the speaker on the cassette. The word is incorrect if it is pronounced as *ánłíí.* The glottal stop must be clearly articulated. Practice saying the 1st and 3rd person forms of this verb as well: *ásh'íí* and *áyiił'íí.*

3. In the Jicarilla negative *doo yá'ásh'íí da* (I am not doing anything), the element *yá* of *iyáná'* (what) precedes the verb *ásh'íí* (I am doing). You will also hear *doo yá' da,* which carries the same meaning.

4. The word *na'íízii* means *you work, are working.* It remains in verb form, with appended enclitic *-yé* when implying the noun *job* in the configuration *he na'íízii'yé dínyá?* (are you going to work?). A verbatim rendition of this question is *(question indicator) you are working toward you are going?*

5. Note that the Jicarilla word *na'íízii,* for *you work,* is distinguished from the 3rd person form *na'iizii* only by tonal difference in the second syllable. Compare Mescalero Apache *na'ńzii* (you work) and Western Apache *na'iiziig* (he works).

6. The interrogative element *ha'* (where) is always followed by a suffixed enclitic. A question in the above dialog contains the term *ha'nǫǫ,* where the enclitic is *-nǫǫ* rather than *-yé* which you learned earlier. As has been noted, *-nǫǫ* is a widely-used enclitic of elusive meaning, serving as a filler or intensifier. It has also been indicated earlier that you will consistently hear *ha'yénǫǫ* and *ha'yéshǫ.*

7. The word *koghǫ* means *home,* and is pronounced *kowǫ.* It is one of the oldest basic nouns in the Apachean languages. *Kǫ* (fire) is combined with the stem *-ghǫ* (home, camp) to provide a meaning approximating *a home where there is fire.* Compare Jicarilla *koghǫ* with Mescalero *ku'wǫ,* and Western Apache *gowǫ.* Navajo *hooghan* has a closely similar stem *-ghan,* but the prefixed element *hoo-* means *space, area, or place,* thus *place home.*

8. *Ńnǫ'ǫ́ǫ́* (your older brother) consists of a high toned possessive pronoun syllabic *n* meaning *your,* singular, and the noun *nǫ'ǫ́ǫ́* (older brother). A few nouns in Jicarilla Apache take high-toned possessive pronouns. Compare low-toned possessive pronouns in *nbíilii* (your car) and *nghǫ* (your home).

9. The term *míízhii* (his, her name) consists of the 3rd person singular possessive pronoun *míí-* and the noun *zhii* (name). Notice again high-toned *míí-.*

10. The interrogative particle *ya* (isn't it, aren't you, etc.) is used in the same manner as in English, e.g., *Háasbila'yé dínyá ya?* (you are going to the hospital, aren't you?) or *Lósii'yé isgwéela nádééh ya?* (he goes to school in Dulce, doesn't he?). Notice

that this particle differs from *yá'* in number 3 above in its low tone and lack of a final glottal stop. Navajo uses low-toned and glottalized *ya'* in a manner identical to Jicarilla Apache *ya*, as in *Chíí wolyée ya'?* (His name is Chii, isn't it?).

Review and practice with new vocabulary

1. Ha'go dá'kwéé (to there) dínyá? — When are you going there?
   Díijíí dá'kwéé déyá — I am going there today.
   Nádeezigo dák'wéé deeyá — She is going there next month.

2. Káził łe' hásht'íí — I want some stew.
   Ts'íiłiłii łe' yííkát'íí — He, she wants some fry-bread.
   He gahée (also *gaée*) łe' hánt'íí? — Do you want some coffee?
   He lósii łe' hánt'íí? — Do you want some candy?

3. Abáachii méońsįį ya? — You are learning Apache, aren't you?
   Mągáanii yéoniisįį ya? — He is learning English, isn't he?

4. Nch'ooníí dá shił hooyéé. — I like your friend.
   He shiich'ooníí dá nił hooyéé? — Do you like my friend?
   Shiishdázha dá mił hooyéé. — He, she likes my younger brother.

5. Mansáana shił likạ. — I like apples *(apples with me they are sweet)*.
   Gahée dá shił likạ'é. — I like coffee.
   He káził dá mił likạ'é? — Does she like stew?

   Note in examples number 4 and 5 above the two distinct ways of expressing *liking*. The term *-ił hooyéé* is used for expressing liking for something other than food, while *-ił likạ* is used exclusively for stating the liking of food and drink, meaning literally *it is sweet with one*. The three 1st person singular postpositions (pronoun and preposition) used with either *hooyéé, gooyéé,* and *likạ* are *shił, nł,* and *mił*. Notice also the use of *dá shił (nł, mił) likạ'é*, slightly intensified forms of *shił (nł, mił) likạ*.

6. Iyáná' há ńnyá? — What did you come for?
   Shiibíilii há néyá. — I came for my car.
   Naałtsoozii yííká ńyá. — She came for the book.

7. He iinłhásh? — Are you going to sleep?
   Aoo, iishhásh. — Yes, I am going to sleep.
   Bíígó iiłhásh. — He too is going to sleep.

17

8. Eełhaash. — I slept.
   He iinłhaash? — Did you sleep?
   Iiłhaash. — He, she slept.

9. Gé sikį́į́. — She is just lying down.
   He gé síinkį́į́? — Are you just lying down?
   Aoo, gé sékį́į́. — Yes, I am just lying down.

10. Nékį́į́. — I lay down.
    He níinkį́į́? — Did you lie down?
    Neskį́į́. — He, she lay down.

11. He ndibé nshé? — Are you shearing your sheep?
    Shiidibé doo hiishé da. — I am not shearing my sheep.
    Bíí shiidibé yishé. — He is shearing my sheep.

12. He dibé ńnshé? — Did you shear the sheep?
    Aoo, dibé héshé. — Yes, I sheared the sheep.
    Dibé yiishé. — He sheared the sheep.

13. He dibé nańyoo? — Are you going to herd sheep?
    Dibé doo naniisoo da. — I am not going to herd sheep.
    Bíí dibé nainiiyoo. — She is going to herd sheep.

14. He dibé nanínyoo? — Did you herd sheep?
    Aoo, dibé nanéyoo. — Yes, I herded sheep.
    Dibé nainesoo. — He herded sheep.

Comprehension practice

Shíí Sam shíízhii. Doo yá'ásh'íí da dákoo, énda dák'adéé na'iisii'yé déyá. Isgwéela'yé na'iisii. Shiina'ą́ą́ Abáachii yéoniisį́į. Díí (*it*, referring to *Abáachii*) dá mił hooyéé. Doo ch'éh áyiił'íí da. Dákoo gahée łe' hásht'íí. Díí (*it*, referring to *gahée*) dá shił łika̧'é.

Questions

1. Hat'éo míízhii? — What is his name?
2. Iyáná' áyiił'íí? — What is he doing?
3. Ha'go na'iizii'yé deeyá? — When is he going to work?
4. Ha'yénáą na'iizii? — Where does he work?

18

5. Miiną'ą́ą́ iyáná' yéoniisįį? — What is his older brother learning?
6. He díí dá mił hooyéé? — Does he like it?
7. He ch'éh áyiił'íí? — Is it difficult for him?
8. Sam iyáná' yííkát'íí? — What does Sam want?
9. Iyáná' dá mił łiką'é? - What does he like?

Expressions

Éíłt'áo. — It is correct.
Doo éíłt'áo da. — It is not correct, it is wrong.
Dá aaníí. — It is true.
Doo aaníí da. — It is not true.
Dá aada'é. — It is far.
Doo aada da. — It is not far.
Aíí! — ouch!

A selective comparison of some Apachean terms

It is muddy. It is cold.

Jicarilla:	Goshtł'ish.	Goosk'as.
Mescalero:	Gushtł'ish.	Guuk'as.
Western:	Goshtł'ish.	Gozk'az.
Navajo:	Hashtł'ish.	Deesk'aaz.

19

Unit 5 ◀◀◀◀

Dialog

Dá nzhǫ́. — Hello, greetings.
Aoo, dá nzhǫ́. — Yes, greetings.

Ha'ánńsį? — How are you?
Doo ánsį. — I am fine.

Ha'shį́į́náą nandá? — Where are you from?
Lósiishį́į́ naashá - I am from Dulce.

He ą́'ee dá gooyéé? — Is it nice there?
Aoo, énda haigo dá goosk'as'é. — Yes, but it is cold in the winter.

He ą́'ee dził góníí? — Are there mountains there?
Aoo, ą́'ee dáłánéé dził góníí — Yes, there are a lot of mountains there.

He ą́'ee zas ntsaa góníí? — Is there much snow there?
Aoo, ą́'ee zas ntsaa haigo — Yes, there is deep (big) snow there in the winter.

Shį́į́goshą? — How is it in the summer (how about the summers)?
Shį́į́go dá goosdo'é — It is hot in the summer,

Vocabulary

1. ha' — where
2. shį́į́ — from
3. ha'shį́į́náą — where from
4. nandá — you walk about, are
5. Lósiishį́į́ — from Dulce, New Mexico
6. naashá — I walk about, am
7. ą́'ee — there
8. dá gooyéé — it is nice, pleasant
9. énda — but
10. haigo — in the winter
11. dá goosk'as'é — it is cold
12. dził — mountain(s)
13. góníí — it exists, they exist
14. dáłánéé — many
15. zas — snow
16. ntsaa — big
17. shį́į́go — in the summer
18. shą — enclitic meaning here, *how about*
19. dá goosdo'é — hot, warm

20

Explanations

1. The suffix *shíí* appended to *ha'* (where) renders *where from*. Added to this, in this dialog, is the enclitic *-náą,* a filler and possible intensifier. The question is also correctly formulated simply as *ha'shíí,* but the native proclivity, as has been indicated, favors frequent use of *-náą,* as in *ha'shíínáą* (where from) as above, and *ha'yénáą* (where to, at where).

2. The 1st and 2nd verbs *naashá* and *nandá* convey the meaning *I walk about, you walk about,* carrying in an idiomatic sense *being from,* when combined with place. Thus, *from Dulce I walk about, I am from Dulce where I walk about, or usually am,* is translated as *Lósiishíí naashá.* Compare with Mescalero *Tsé Táyesi'áshíí ásht'íí* (I am (generically) from Ruidoso) and Navajo *Na'nízhoozhídéé' naashá* (I am (I walk about) from Gallup).

3. *Gooyéé* and *dá gooyéé* mean *it is nice, pleasant,* usually in reference to a place. Remember that when preceded by *shił, nił (nł), mił* the meanings *I like it, you like it, he, she likes it* are rendered.

4. *Haigo* (in the winter) has the components *hai* (winter) and *-go,* an enclitic which conveys the sense of *when* or *it being.*

5. The word *goosk'as* means *it is cold.* It is common in Jicarilla Apache to intensify or color the expression with prepounded *dá* and postpounded *'é,* hence *dá goosk'as'é.* *Goosk'as* and *goosdo* (it is hot) refer to amospheric temperature. For food, drink, or other objects *sik'as* or *sido* must be used, as in *káził dá sik'as'é* (the stew is cold), or *gahée dá sido'é* (the coffee is hot).

6. *Góníí* means *it exists, they exist.* Thus, *dził góníí* translates as *there is a mountain, there are mountains.* As has been explained previously, *góníí,* with 1st, 2nd, and 3rd person possessive pronouns prefixed to a noun, render the meaning *I have, you have, he, she has,* e.g., *shiilíí' góníí* (I have a horse).

7. *Zas ntsaa* translates literally as *snow big.* Also used is *zas diką* (thick or deep snow). *Zas* is the common word for *snow* among the various Apache linguistic groups. Navajo uses *yas,* except for eastern Navajos who seem to favor *zas.* Compare the phrase with Navajo *yas ntsaa* and *yas ditą.*

8. *Dá goosdo'é* means *it is quite hot,* in reference to the atmosphere. See number 5 above.

9. *Shíígo* is translated as *in the summer* (see number 4 above). The enclitic *-shą* is the

21

equivalent of *how about*. Compare *shíígo* with *shíígó ąą* (I too, I also, where *ąą* is a filler with no separate meaning) in number 2 below.

Review and practice with new vocabulary

1. Ha'shíínąą naaghá? — Where is he from?
   Chama'shíí naaghá. — He is from Chama.

2. Dííshą, ha'shíí nandá? — How about you, where are you from?
   Shíígó ąą, Chama'shíí naashá. — I too am from Chama.

3. He ą'ee dáłánéé diidé góníí? — Are there a lot of people there?
   Dooda, doo dáłánéé da. — No, not many.

4. He gahée dá sido'é? — Is the coffee hot?
   Aoo, dá sido'é. — Yes, it is hot.

5. He nka'éé domáadii łe' yííkát'íí? — Does your father want some tomatoes?
   Dooda, béela łe' yííkát'íí. — No, he wants some pears.

6. He déeh łe' hánt'íí? — Do you want some tea?
   Dooda, dáan łe' hásht'íí. — No, I want some food.

7. He įį'ee dáan łe' góníí? — Is there some food here?
   Aoo, įį'ee naa'oléé shíí łeet'áan łe' góníí. — Yes, there are beans and some bread here.

8. Díí adóolii dá łikạ'é. — This corn meal mush is tasty.
   Aoo, dá shił łikạ'é. — Yes, I like it.

9. He įį'ee naaltsoozii łe' góníí?   Are there some books (paper(s)) here?
   He įį'ee zháał łe' góníí? — Is there some money here?
   Aoo, įį'ee łe' góníí. — Yes, there is some here.

10. He ndibé góníí? — Do you have sheep?
    Aoo, shiidibézháá łe' góníí — Yes, I have some lambs.

11. Nyii'ííshą, he miidibé góníí? — How about your son, does he have sheep?
    Dooda, miidibé édįį, énda miiłíí' łe' góníí. — No, he has no sheep, but he has some horses.

12. Dá'kwíí miilį́į'? — How many horses does he have (how many his horses)?
    Dáłaa'é miilį́į'. — He has one horse (one his horse).
    Shiika'éé naakii miibóó. — My father has two cows.
    Shii'máá kái'ii miichíníí. — My mother has three dogs.
    Shiihaskįįyíí dį́į'ii miidibé. — My husband has four sheep.
    Shii'á ashdle' miimósha. — My wife has five cats.

    Note above that *miilį́į'* (his, her horse) is the possessed form, with voiced *l* and glottal
    stop. The unpossessed form for *horse* is *łį́į,* with unvoiced *l* (*ł*) and no glottal stop.

13. He zas nagoołkįįh? — Is it snowing?
    Aoo, zas nagoołkįįh. — Yes, it is snowing.
    Zas nááłką́. — It snowed.
    Zas nagóółką́. — It stopped snowing.

14. Nzhách'į'íí iyáná' áyiił'íí? — What is your daughter doing?
    Shiizhách'į'íí dénda'yé na'iizii. — My daughter is working at the store.

15. Díísha, he na'íízii'yé dínyá? — How about you, are you going to work?
    Aoo, dákoo déyá. — Yes, I am going now.

16. He kósiłká'yé na'íízii? — Do you work at the lake?
    Dooda, įį'ee na'iisii. — No, I work right here.

17. He įį'ee dá nł gooyéé? — Do you like it here?
    Aoo, dá shił gooyéé. — Yes, I like it.

Comprehension

Shíí Mary shíízhii. Lósiishį́í naashá. Á'ee dá gooyéé, énda haigo dá goosk'as'é. Á'ee
dził góníí. Haigo zas ntsaa góníí. Shį́įgo dá goosdo'é á'ee. Dákoo doo yá'ásh'íí da, énda
dák'adéé na'iisii'yé déyá. Háasbila'yé na'iisii.

Questions

1. Hat'éo míízhii? — What is her name?
2. Ha'shį́í naaghá? — Where is she from?
3. He á'ee dá gooyéé? — Is it nice there?
4. He á'ee dził góníí? — Are there mountains there?

5. He haigo á'ee dá goosk'as'é? — Is it cold there in the winter?
6. He zas ntsaa góníí á'ee? — Is there a lot of snow there?
7. He shíígo á'ee dá goosdo'é? — Is it warm there in the summer?
8. Dákoo iyáná' áyiił'íí? — What is she doing now?
9. Ha'yé deesyá? — Where is she going?
10. Ha'go dá'kwéé deesyá? — When is she going there?
11. Ha'yé na'iizii? — Where does she work?

Expressions and questions

Hat'énáą ándzaa? — What happened to you?
Ńlanáą hat'é ádzaa? — What happened to your hand?
Shííla shégish. — I cut my hand.
Hóch'ishí. — Come here, this way.
Ye' iindééh. — Come in.
Ye' iindééh gótsaa. — Come in, there is lots of room (big space).
Dah ńdei. — Sit down.
He nee ńnłdeh? — Are you tired?
Aoo, nee néłdeh. — Yes, I am tired.
Shił goosk'as. — I am cold.
Shił goosdo. — I am warm (also, *I am drunk*).
K'adii. — Let's go.

A selective comparison of some Apachean terms

Where are you from?

Jicarilla: Ha'shíí nandá?
Mescalero: Ha'shíí áńt'íí?
Western: Hayé' nadaa?
Navajo: Háádę́ę́' naniná?

24

Unit 6 ◀◀◀◀

Dialog

He Abáachii k'eh yánłkii? — Do you speak Apache?
Aoo, nzhǫ́go k'eh yáshkii. — Yes, I speak it well.

Naakaiiyéé miizaashą? — How about the Spanish language?
Dooda, doo k'eh yáshkii da. — No, I don't speak it.

Mągáaniishą? — How about English?
Ałts'íísdéo k'eh yáshkii. — I speak it a little.

He ndádéé Abáachii k'eh yáłkii? — Does your older sister speak Apache?
Doo nzhǫ́go k'eh yáłkii. — She does not speak it well.

Abáachii méoniisįį hásht'įį. I want to learn Apache.
Shiich'oondé. — Help me.
Aoo, nch'ooshdé. — Yes, I will help you.

Vocabulary

1. Abáachii k'eh — in the Apache manner or way
2. yánłkii — you speak
3. nzhǫ́go — well (adverb)
4. yáshkii — I speak
5. Naakaiiyéé — Spanish
6. miizaa — his, her, their language
7. Mągáanii — White Man, English
8. ałts'íísdéo — a little bit (adverb)
9. dádéé — older sister
10. ndádéé — your older sister
11. yáłkii — he, she speaks it
12. méoniisįį — I am learning it

Explanations

1. *K'eh* means *in the manner of, like*. Thus, *Abáachii k'eh yáshkii* means literally *Apache in the manner of I speak*. *K'eh* is echoed in Navajo *k'eh,* with the same meaning, as in *dinék'eh* (in the Navajo way), or with Mescalero *Ndee bik'eyu yáshti* (I speak Mescalero Apache).

25

2. The word *nzhǫ́* means *it is good, nice, beautiful.* When the enclitic *-go* is appended to it, it is adverbialized as *nzhǫ́go,* rendering the meaning *well.*

3. *Naakaiiyéé* (Spanish), is the 3rd person plural verb form meaning *they who wander about, they who walk about,* probably in reference to the mobility of the Spanish *conquistadores.*

4. *Naakaiiyéé miizaa* translates literally as *they who wander about — their language,* i.e., *the Spanish language.* In this configuration *mii-* is the 3rd person plural possessive pronoun and *zaa* (the possessed form of *saa*) means *language.*

5. The noun *Mǫgáanii* (white person, English language) is derived from Spanish *americano, americana.*

6. *Álts'íísdéo* is a slightly shortened form of *álts'íísdégo.* In Jicarilla Apache speech the *g-* of the adverbializing enclitic *-go* is commonly omitted.

7. *Ndádéé* (your older sister) may be compared with Navajo *nádí.*

8. In previous units you have had some experience with the verb *to want* (hásht'íí, hánt'íí, yííkát'íí) when used with nouns. To express *want* or *wish* with a verb in the present tense, simply use the given imperfective (present tense) verb person and follow it with the appropriate person of the Apache verb *to want,* e.g., *Abáachii k'eh yáshkii* (I speak Apache) *hásht'íí* (I want), I want to speak Apache; or *na'iizii yííkát'íí,* he, she wants to work. Another way of expressing wish or wanting with a verb is the use of the enclitic *-go* appended to the first verb: *Na'iisiigo hásht'íí* (I want to work). Both usages are current in everyday Jicarilla Apache speech.

More examples:

Iṣgwéclu náṣhdę́ę́h(go) húṣht'íí.   I want to attend school.
Chama'yé déyá(go) yííkát'íí. — He wants to go to Chama.
He Abáachii diints'e(go) hánt'íí? — Do you want to understand Apache?

Review and practice with new vocabulary

1. He Inłt'ánéé k'eh yánłkii? — Do you speak Navajo?
    Dooda, Nadaíin k'eh yáshkii. — No, I speak Mescalero Apache.
    Dawoséeo k'eh yáshkii. — I speak Taos.
    Yóda k'eh yáshkii. — I speak Ute.

2. Iyáná' k'eh yáłkii? — What does he speak?
    Łeeshchíí k'eh yáłkii. — He speaks Western Apache.
    Mągáanii miizaa k'eh yáłkii. — He speaks the English language.
    Yóda miizaa k'eh yáłkii. — She speaks the Ute language.

3. He Abáachii nzhǫ́go k'eh yánłkii? — Do you speak Apache well?
    Abáachii áłts'íísdéo k'eh yáshkii. — I speak a little Apache.

4. He Abáachii méońsįįgo hánt'įį? — Do you want to learn Apache?
    Aoo, méoniisįįgo hásht'įį. — Yes, I want to learn it.
    Diists'e hásht'įį. — I want to understand it.

5. He dá bíneendlįį? — Are you interested in it?
    Dá míneeshłįį. — I am interested in it.
    Dá yéneedlįį. — He, she is interested in it.

6. Iyáná' ánł'įį hánt'įį? — What do you want to do?
    Ishą́ hásht'įį. — I want to eat.
    Ishdlą́ hásht'įį — I want to drink.
    Óshkai hásht'įį — I want to read.
    Ishhosh hásht'įį — I want to sleep.

7. Ha'shį́įną́ą nandá? — Where are you from?
    Abáachii miikéyaashį́į naashá? — I am from the Apache reservation (*Abáachii miikéyaa*: Apache their land).

8. Ha'shį́įną́ą naaghá? — Where is she from?
    Yóda miikéyaashį́į naaghá. — She is from the Ute reservation
    Nadaíin miikéyaashį́į naaghá. — She is from the Mescalero reservation.

9. He ą́'ee shash góníí? — Are there bears there?
    Aoo, dziłyé shash góníí. — Yes, in the mountains there are bears.

10. Ą́'ee bįį góníí. — There are deer there.
    Įį'ee ba'iitso góníí. — There are wolves here.
    Ą́'ee shǫ́ǫdii góníí. — There are coyote there.
    Įį'ee itsá góníí. — There are eagles here.
    Ą́'ee gáagee góníí. — There are crows there.
    Įį'ee naał'eełéé góníí. — There are ducks here.

11. Dá'kwíí n'íłchíń? — How many children do you have?
    Goskáan shii'íłchíń. — I have six children.

27

Gosts'idii shii'iłchíń. — I have seven children.
Tseebíí shiilį́į'. — I have eight horses.
Nóóst'éí shiidibé. — I have nine sheep.
Goneesnáan shiibóó. — I have ten cows.

Comprehension

Shiiyii'į́į́ Abáachii doo nzhǫ́go k'eh yáłkii da. Áń yéoniisįį yííkát'į́į́.
Abáachii dá yéneedlį́į́. Dá mił hooyéé. Áń Mǫgáanii miizaa nzhǫ́go k'eh yáłkii.
Shiidádéé Abáachii shį́į́ Inłt'ánéé áłts'íísdéo k'eh yáłkii.
Inłt'ánéé miikéyaa'yé na'iizii, énda Lósii'yé na'iizii yííkát'į́į́.

Questions

1. He miiyįį'į́į́ Abáachii nzhǫ́go k'eh yáłkii? — Does his, her son speak Apache well?
2. He áń yéoniisįį yííkát'į́į́? — Does he want to learn it?
3. Iyáná' dá yéneedlį́į́? — What interests him?
4. Iyáná' nzhǫ́go k'eh yáłkii? — What does he speak well?
5. Miidádéé iyáná' k'eh yáłkii? — What does his, her older sister speak?
6. Miidádéé ha'yé na'iizii? — Where does his, her older sister work?
7. Ha'yé na'iizii yííkát'į́į́? — Where does she want to work?

Expressions

Doo shaa nínt'į́į́. — Don't bother me.
Doo gońyą́! — You blockhead! (You are not smart).
Doo góyą́. — He, she is stupid.
Doo gonsą́. — I am so dumb.

Adjectives

1. Kóh sido. —The water is warm.
2. Gahée sik'as. —The coffee is cold.
3. Káził shiibéésh. — The stew is boiled.
4. Tł'é'na'áí łiijooł. — The moon is round.
5. Tł'ó'yé gótǫ́ǫ́'é. — The weather is bad (outside it is bad).
6. Ísee dá ndaazé. — The pot is heavy.
7. Naałtsoozii ászóólé. — The book is light.

Cultural Note

The formality of saying *please* is not practiced by the Jicarilla Apache when they speak their own language. It is inferred that when a simple request is made, it will be acceded to. In the Apache way of thinking there is no need to plead or beg. The Jicarilla equivalent *nooshkałee,* as well as Western Apache *noshkąąh* and Navajo *t'áá shǫǫdí,* express the idea of *please,* but are only used in imploring. Therefore, *kázil łe' hásht'íí* (I want some stew) or *shich'oondé* (help me) suffice.

A selective comparison of some Apachean terms

I speak Apache (Navajo).

Jicarilla: Abáachii k'eh yáshkii.
Mescalero: Ndee bik'eyu yáshti.
Western: Ndee (or *nnee*) k'ehgo yáshti'.
Navajo: Dinék'ehjí yáshti'.

Unit 7 ◀◀◀◀

Dialog

He kéesda'yé nasínyá? — Did you go to the feast?
Aoo, dá'kwéé naséyá. Yes, I went there.

Nka'éeshą, he dá'kwéé naasyá? — How about your father, did he go?
Dooda, doo dá'kwéé naasyá da. — No, he didn't go there.
Na'iizii ńt'éé. — He was working.

Iyáná' yee na'iizii? — What is his work?
Dáan áyił'íí'íí nilíí. — He is a cook.
Háasbila'yé na'iizii. — He works at a hospital.

He n'máá kéesda'yé naasyá? — Did your mother go to the feast?
Aoo, dá'kwéé naasyá. — Yes, she went there.

Vocabulary

1. kéesda — feast
2. nasínyá — you went
3. naséyá — I went
4. nka'éé — your father
5. dá'kwéé — there
6. na'iizii — he, she is working
7. ńt'éé — past tense indicator
8. na'iizii ńt'éé — he was working
9. iyáná' — what
10. yee — with, by means of
11. na'iizii — he works
12. dáan áyiił'íí'íí — a cook, cooks
13. nilíí — he, she is
14. háasbila — hospital
15. n'máá — your mother
16. naasyá — he, she went

Explanations

1. The perfective mode, which indicates completed action, is equivalent to English past tense. Thus *naséyá* means *I went (and returned)*. *Nasínyá* and *naasyá* are the perfective 2nd and 3rd person singular forms of this verb.

2. The term *nka'éé* (your father) consists of syllabic *n*, representing the second person possessive pronoun (your), and *-ka'éé* (father). The other two singular forms are *shiika'éé* (my father) and *miika'éé* (his, her father). Compare 1st person Mescalero, Western Apache and Navajo *shitaa'*.

3. The word *ńt'éé* is used following an imperfective verb (present tense, action not completed) to signify past time, *used to, was*. Thus, *na'iizii ńt'éé* translates literally as *he is working was*, i.e., *he was working*. It follows that 1st person *na'iisii ńt'éé* is translated as *I was working*.

4. The first three persons singular of the neuter verb *to be* are *nishłį́į́, ńłį́į́, and nilį́į́*, translated as *I am, you are, he, she is*.

5. *Dáan áyiił'į́į́'ii* (cook) is comprised of the noun *dáan* (food), *áyiił'į́į́* (he, she makes or prepares it), and the relativizing enclitic *-íí* (one who). Thus, *one who prepares food* is rendered. The person of the verb *to be* (*nishłį́į́, ńłį́į́, nilį́į́*) matches the person expressed in the verb *to make, prepare* (*ásh'į́į́, ánł'į́į́, áyiił'į́į́*) when a statement of occupation is made, for example, *dáan ásh'į́į́'íí nishłį́į́* (I am a cook), *dáan ánł'į́į́'íí ńłį́į́* (you are a cook), and so on.

6. *Háasbila* is obviously derived from English *hospital*. Although Jicarilla Apache borrows relatively few words from Indo-European languages, more are drawn from Spanish than from English.

7. *N'máá* combines the 2nd person possessive syllabic *n* with the noun *máá*. In this particular conjunction a glottal stop separates the possessive pronoun and the noun. The three persons in the singular are *shii'máá, n'máá,* and *mii'máá*, i.e, *my mother, your mother, his, her mother*. Compare Mescalero and Navajo *shimá* and Western Apache *shimaa*.

Review and practice with new vocabulary

1. Ha'yénáá nasínyá? — Where did you go?
   Ináaso'yé naséyá — I went to Ignacio (Ignacio, Colorado).

2. N'máá ha'yénáá naasyá? — Where did your mother go?
   Ík'áá'yé naasyá. — She went to the hills.

3. Iyáná' yee na'iizii? — What is his, her work?
   Kįį áyiił'į́į́'íí nilį́į́. — He, she is a carpenter.

31

4. He dáan ánł'íí'íí ńlį́į́? — Are you a cook?
   Iizee ásh'íí'íí nishłį́į́. — I am a nurse.

5. Iyáná' yee na'iizii ńt'éé? — What did his work used to be?
   Wées (Sp. *juez*) nilį́į́ ńt'éé. — He used to be a judge.

6. He yidóoł ńlį́į́? — Are you a doctor?
   Segidéeł nishłį́į́. — I am a secretary.

7. Ntsóóyéé iyáná' yee na'iizii? — What is your grandfather's work?
   Haskįįyíí gokaałii nilį́į́. — He is a medicine man.

8. Nant'áan nilį́į́. — He is the leader.
   Nahiinant'áan nilį́į́. — He is our tribal leader.

Comprehension

Kéesda'yé naséyá. Shiika'éé gó (also) dá'kwéé naasyá, énda shii'máá doo naasyá da.
Na'iizii ńt'éé. Éí (*she,* referring to *shii'máá*) segidéeł nilį́į́. Háasbila'yé na'iizii. Á'ee
na'iiziigo dá mił hooyéé.

Questions

1. Ha'yénáá naasyá? — Where did he, she go?
2. He miika'éé gó dá'kwéé naasyá? — Did his father also go there?
3. He mii'máá dá'kwéé naasyá? — Did his mother go there?
4. He mii'máá na'iizii ńt'éé? — Was his mother working?
5. Mii'máá iyáná' yee na'iizii? — What is his mother's work?
6. Mii'máá ha'yénáá na'iizii? — Where does his mother work?
7. Háasbila'yé na'iiziigo dá mił hooyéé? — Does she like working in a hospital?

Expressions

Gé ádiishníí. — I am just kidding.
Doo mégosį da. — I don't know.
Inłt'ánéé doo mégosį da. — I don't know Navajo.
Abáachii mégosį. — I know Apache.
Íłtsé. — Wait.

Áńáá dńíí. — Repeat it.

Chįį she'yiiłhį́įh. — I am hungry (hunger is killing me).

Bá she'yiiłhį́įh. — I am thirsty (thirst is killing me).

Cultural Note

It is believed that the designation *Apache* is derived from the Zuni word *Abachu,*
meaning *enemy,* a term originally applied by the Zuni to the Navajo and, by extension,
to the Apache. Both the Western Apache term *Nasht'ízhé* and the Navajo word
Naasht'ézhí, the expression in each of those languages for the Zuni, are translated as
charcoal-blackened enemy, in reference to the Zuni custom of blackening the bodies of
their warriors with charcoal. It is interesting that the Jicarillas call the Navajo *Inłt'ánéé,*
a term which means *those who grow things,* referring to the early Navajo proclivity for
agriculture. The 3rd person Navajo verb form for *to raise it, to grow it, to mature it* is
yiniłt'á. The correspondence between Navajo *-niłt'á* and Jicarilla Apache *-nłt'ánéé* can
clearly be seen.

A selective comparison of some Apachean terms

I am hungry. I am thirsty.

Jicarilla:	Chįį she'yiiłhį́įh. Bá she'yiiłhį́įh.
Mescalero:	Dachį shiye'esxį́įh. Dabá' sheye'esxį́įh.
Western:	Shidá' nishłį́į. Dibá' nishłį́į.
Navajo:	Dichin shi'niiłhį́. Dibáá' shi'niiłhį́.
	Dichin nishłį́. Dibáá' nishłį́.

Unit 8 ◀◀◀◀

Dialog

Ha'yénáá nasínyá? — Where did you go?
Dziłntsaa'yé naséyá. — I went to Albuquerque.

Hat'éonáá nasínyá? — How (by what means) did you go?
Shiibíilii mee naséyá. — I went in my car.

Dá'kwéé shił ń'ash. — Take me there.
Aoo, dá'kwéé nł diish'ash. — Yes, I'll take you there.

Ashdle' béeso bik'édéé na'ńléego dá'kwéé nł diish'ash — I'll take you there for five dollars.

He nzháalii góníí? — Do you have any money?
Dooda, shiizháalii édįį. — No, I have no money.

Haéé'ą, dá'kwéé diit'ash. — All right, let's go there.
Ihéedń — Thank you.

Vocabulary

1. ha'yénáá — where to
2. nasínyá — you went
3. Dziłntsaa — Albuquerque, New Mexico
4. naséyá — I went
5. hat'éonáá — how, by what means
6. shiibíilii — my car
7. mee — by means of it
8. shił — with me
9. ń'ash — you (and I) will go
10. nił (nł) — with you
11. diish'ash — I (and you) will go
12. ashdle' béeso — five dollars
13. bik'édéé — for, in exchange for
14. na'ńléego — when payment ıs made
15. he — question indicator
16. nzháalii — your money
17. góníí — it exists
18. shiizháalii — my money
19. édįį — it does not exist
20. haéé'ą — all right
21. diit'ash — let's (the two of us) go

34

Explanations

1. The Jicarilla word for Albuquerque, *Dziłntsaa,* means *big mountain,* in reference to the massive Sandia Mountains east of the city.

2. *Hat'éonąą* (how, by what means) is a short form for *hat'égonąą.* As explained earlier, the appended enclitic *-nąą* is widely used in Jicarilla Apache discourse. It is an emphatic, or filler, of indefinable meaning as a separate or single element.

3. *Shiibíilii mee naséyá* translates literally as *my car by means of it (with it) I went.* With a coincidence of third person subject and object, such as in the statement *miibíilii yee naasyá* (she went in her car), note that the postposition *mee* changes to *yee.*

4. In the expression *dá'kwéé shił ń'ash* (take me there), the word *shił* means *with me,* and *ń'ash* is composed of high-toned syllabic *ń* (you, singular) and the 2nd person dual verb stem *-'ash* (two go). A literal rendition of the phrase is *there with me you we (two) go.* Similarly, when 1st and 2nd persons are switched, as in *dá'kwéé nł diish'ash* (I will take you there), *nł* signifies *with you* and *diish'ash* consists of 1st person singular future marker *diish-* and again the 2nd person dual verb stem *-'ash.* Thus, the phrase is translated literally as *there with you I shall (we two) go.* In these examples both the one accompanying and the one accompanied are singular. The verb stem *-'ash* is dual and reflects the involvement of both singular subject and singular object in the action. These structures are closely comparable to Navajo *shił díí'ash* and *nił deesh'ash.*

5. The word *béeso* (dollar) is from Spanish *peso.*

6. *Bik'édéé na'ńléego* may be rendered as *in exchange for payment of.*

7. *Édįį* means *it does not exist.* Contrast it with *góníí* (it exists) and use it to express non-possession: *shiibíilii édįį* (I have no car), i.e., *my car it does not exist.* It also signifies that *he, she, it is dead (or absent),* e.g., *shiitsóóyéé édįį* (my grandfather is deceased). This term compares closely with Mescalero Apache *édįį* and Navajo *ádin.*

Review and practice with new vocabulary

1. He Dziłntsaa'yé dínyá? — Are you going to Albuquerque?
   Dooda, doo dá'kwéé déyá da. — No, I am not going there.

2. He Ináaso'yé naasyá? — Did he go to Ignacio?
   Dooda, doo dá'kwéé naasyá da. — No, he didn't go there.

3. Ha'dą́ kéesda'yé naasyá? — When did she go to the feast?
   Shį́į́dą́ dá'kwéé naasyá. — She went there last summer.

4. He miibíilii yee naasyá? — Did she go in her car?
   Dooda, bąąs yee naasyá. — No, she went by wagon.
   Naat'a'íí mee naséyá. — I went by airplane.

5. Lósii'yé déyágo hásht'į́į. — I want to go to Dulce.
   Dá'kwéé nł diish'ash. — I'll take you there.

6. He nlį́į' góníí? — Do you have a horse (horses)?
   Shiilį́į' édįį. — I do not have a horse (horses).

7. Blanco'yé shił ń'ash. — Take me to Blanco.
   Aoo, nł diish'ash. — Yes, I'll take you.
   Dá'kwéé diit'ash. — Let's go there.

8. He n'máá segidéeł nilį́į? — Is your mother a secretary?
   Dooda, má'ółkai'íí nilį́į. — No, she is a teacher.

9. He nka'éé háasbila'yé na'iizii ńt'éé? — Was your father working at the hospital?
   Isgwéela'yé na'iizii ńt'éé. — He was working at the school.

10. Chįį she'yiiłhį́į́h. He dáan łe' góníí? — I'm hungry. Is there some food?
    Aoo, ts'íłłłii shį́į́ káził góníí. — Yes, there is fry bread and stew.

11. He bá ne'yiiłhį́į́h? — Are you thirsty?
    Aoo, bá she'yiiłhį́į́h. He kólichíí'íí góníí? — Yes, I am thirsty. Is there soda pop?

12. He Abáachii méońsįįgo hánt'į́į? — Do you want to learn Apache?
    Aoo, éí k'eh yáshkiigo hásht'į́į. — Yes, I want to speak it.

13. He zas nagoołkįįh? — Is it snowing?
    Dooda, nagoołkįįh. — No, it is raining.

14. He zas nagóółką́? — Did it snow?
    Dooda, nagóółką́. — No, it rained.

15. He zas nááłhį́į́h? — Is the snow melting?
    Aoo, zas nááłhį́į́h. — Yes, the snow is melting.

16. Godiłkǫǫh. — It is slippery.
    Nzhǫ́go nandá! — Be careful!

More numerals

łats'áadiih mósha — eleven cats
naakiits'áadiih chíníí — twelve dogs
káts'áadiih bóó — thirteen cows
dííts'áadiih łį́į́' — fourteen horses
ashdlats'áadiih gah — fifteen rabbits
goskáants'áadiih shash — sixteen bears
gosts'its'áadiih bįį — seventeen deer
tseebííts'áadiih shǫ́ǫdii — eighteen coyotes
nóóst'éíts'áadiih iyánéé — nineteen buffalo
naadin dlǫ́' — twenty prairie dogs

Comprehension

Dziłntsaa'yé naséyá. Á'ee dá shił gooyéé. Shiibíilii mee dá'kwéé naséyá. Dziłntsaa'yé zas nagóółką́. Shiishdázha á'ee miigha. Á'ee háasbila'yé na'iizii. Éí yidóoł nilį́į́.

Questions

1. Ha'yénáą naasyá? — Where did she (he) go?
2. He á'ee dá mił gooyéé? — Does she like it there?
3. Hat'éonáą dá'kwéé yee naasyá? — How did she go there?
4. He á'ee zas nagóółką́? — Did it snow there?
5. Miishdázha ha'yé miigha? — Where does her younger brother live?
6. Miishdázha ha'yé na'iizii? — Where does her brother work?
7. Iyáná' yee na'iizii? — What is his work?
8. He miishdázha yidóoł nilį́į́? — Is her brother a doctor?

Expressions

He gé ádníí? — Are you kidding?
Aoo, gé ádiishníí. — Yes, I am just kidding.
Nówoch'į! — Scram!
Nówoch'į nandá! — Go away!

Cultural note

Most currency designations in Jicarilla Apache are derived from Spanish:

béeso — peso
sindáo — centavo
zháał — real

A selective comparison of some Apachean terms

It is raining.

Jicarilla: Nagoołkįįh.
Mescalero: Naałtįįh.
Western: Nagołtįh.
Navajo: Nahałtin.

Unit 9 ◀◀◀◀

Dialog

Ha'yé nghạ? — Where is your home?
Ịị'eeshị́ị́ shádii'áí'yéo shiighạ. — My home is south of here.
Ịị'eeshị́ị́ shá'ii'áí'yéo shiighạ. — My home is west of here.

Díishạ, ha'yénáạ nghạ? — How about you, where is your home?
Lósiishị́ị́ sháha'áí'yéo shiighạ. My home is east of Dulce.
Chamashị́ị́ náakosii'yéo shiighạ. My home is north of Chama.

Ha'dạ́ dziłyé nasínyá? — When did you go to the mountains?
Adạ́dạ́ dá'kwéé naséyá. — I went there yesterday.

Ha'ń ạ́'ee hiinłtsạ́? — Whom did you see there?
Shiichóó heełtsạ́. — I saw my grandmother.

Vocabulary

1. ha'yé — where (at where)
2. nghạ — your home
3. ịị'eeshị́ị́ — from here
4. shádii'áí — south
5. shádii'áí'yéo — to the south
6. shá'ii'áí — west
7. shá'ii'áí'yéo — to the west
8. shiighạ — my home
9. díishạ — how about you
10. ha'yénáạ — where (at where)
11. Lósiishị́ị́ — from Dulce
12. náakosii — north
13. náakosii'yéo — to the north
14. sháha'áí — east
15. sháha'áí'yéo — to the east
16. ha'dạ́ — when (past time only)
17. dziłyé — to the mountains
18. nasínyá — you went
19. adạ́dạ́ — yesterday
20. dá'kwéé — there (to there)
21. naséyá — I went
22. ha'ń — who, whom
23. ạ́'ee — there (at there)
24. hiinłtsạ́ — you saw
25. shiichóó — my grandmother
26. heełtsạ́ — I saw

Explanations

1. *Ii'eeshíí* (from here) is constituted of the word *ii'ee* (here) and the enclitic *-shíí* (from).

2. The word *shádii'áí* (south) consists of the element *shá* (sun), the inceptive particle *-dii-*, signifying the beginning of an action, and the verb stem *-'áí*, imparting the concept of a roundish or bulky object (in this case the sun) being moved, carried, or handled. Thus, idiomatically speaking, the sun begins to be carried or starts to move.

3. *Shá'ii'áí* (west), containing the element *-'ii'-* (away out of sight), conveys the concept of the sun, a roundish object, moving away out of sight or setting.

4. The term *sháha'áí* (east) contains the defining element *-ha-* (up, upward) contributing to the literal meaning of a roundish object moving upward, sunrise.

5. The word *náakosii* (north) carries the literal meaning *it revolves, it turns,* in reference to The Big Dipper. Compare this term with Western Apache *náhokosé* and Navajo *náhookọs,* the appelations in both languages for the constellation Ursa Major.

6. The elements *-yégo* (*-yé* = toward; *-go* = being) appended to the cardinal directions convey the idiomatic meaning *to, toward: náakosii'yégo* (to the north). In normal speech such a combination is usually pronounced *náakosii'yéo,* and is displayed as such in this unit.

7. The enclitic *-shíí,* meaning *from,* is suffixed to nouns or adverbs: *Lósiishíí* (from Dulce); *ii'eeshíí* (from here); *á'eeshíí* (from there). Contrast Jicarilla *-shíí* with Mescalero *-shíí,* Western Apache *-yé', -gé', -dí'* and Navajo *-dóó, -déé'. Nota bene: shíí* also means *and,* as well as *probably,* in Jicarilla Apache.

8. The enclitic *-dá* is a marker of past time: *ha'dá* (when); *adádá* (yesterday); *naakiiskádá* (two days ago) You will remember that *ha'go* (when) is used to ask about future time.

9. The three persons singular of the verb *to see* are *heełtsá, hiinłtsá, yiiłtsá.* Note that the 3rd person verb *hiiłtsá* means *she is pregnant.*

Review and practice with new vocabulary

1. Ha'yénáá nahiighą? — Where is your (plural) home?
   Kwéé nahiighą. — Our home is here.

40

2. Ha'yénąą miighą? — Where is his home?
   Ąch'į miighą. — His home is over there.

3. Nghąshą? — How about your home?
   Dziłshíí náakosii'yéo shiighą. — My home is north of the mountain.
   Nghąshíí shádii'áí'yéo shiighą. — My home is south of your home.

4. Miighąshą? — How about his (their) home?
   Shiighąshíí shá'ii'áí'yéo miigha. — His home is west of my home.

5. Ha'yénąą nahiighą? — Where is your (plural) home?
   Nahiighąshíí sháha'áí'yéo nahiighą. — Our home is east of your home.

6. He n'máá hiinłtsą́? — Did you see you mother?
   Shii'máá shíí shiika'éé heełtsą́. — I saw my mother and my father.

7. He nahiibíilii hiinłtsą́? — Did you see our car?
   Dooda, éí doo heełtsą́ da. — No, I did not see it.

8. Iyáná' méońsįį ńt'éé? — What were you learning?
   Abáachii méoniisįį ńt'éé. — I was learning Apache.

9. He na'íízii ńt'éé? — Did you used to work?
   Aoo, isgwéela'ee na'iisii ńt'éé. — Yes, I used to work at a school.

10. Shiibéeso góníí ńt'éé. — I used to have money.
    Shiibíilii góníí ńt'éé, dákoo édįį — I used to have a car, but not now.

11. Dá goosdo'é ya? — It is hot, isn't it?
    Aoo, dá shił goosdo'é. — Yes, I am hot.

12. Kįį'yé dínyá ya? — You are going to the store, aren't you?
    Dooda, doo dá'kwéé déyá da. — No, I am not going there.

13. Zas nagoołkįįh ya? — It is snowing, isn't it?
    Aoo, zas ntsaa góníí. — Yes, there is a lot of snow.

14. Dá aada'é ya? — It is far, isn't it?
    Dooda, áháánéé. — No, it is nearby.

15. Iyáná'ííká dá'kwéé dínyá? — Why are you going there?
    Ą́'ee dá shił gooyéé. — I like it there.

41

16. Iyáná'ííká méońsįį? — Why are you learning it?
    Dá míneeshłį́į. — I am interested in it.

17. Iyáná'ííká ą́'ee na'iizii? — Why is she working there?
    Ą́'ee dá mił gooyéé. — She likes it there.

18. Ha'yé naasyá? — Where did he go?
    Dziłntsaa'yé naasyá. — He went to Albuquerque.

19. Hat'éoną́ą dá'kwéé yee naasyá? — How did he go there?
    Bį́ił yee naasyá. — He went by car.

Comprehension

Shíí Jim shíízhii. Shiighą į̇'eeshį́í doo aada da. Lósiishį́í náakosii'yéo shiighą. Ą́'ee dá shił gooyéé. Shiighąshį́í sháha'áí'yéo shii'máá miighą. Adą́dą́ Ináaso'yé naséyá. Ą́ch'į shiichóó heełtsą́.

Questions

1. Hat'éo míízhii? — What is his name?
2. He miighą į̇'eeshį́í dá aada'é? — Is his home far from here?
3. Lósiishį́í ha'yéo miighą? — What direction is his home from Dulce?
4. He ą́'ee dá mił gooyéé? — Does he like it there?
5. Adą́dą́ ha'yéną́ą naasyá? — Where did he go yesterday?
6. Ą́ch'į ha'ń yiiłtsą́? — Whom did he see there?

Expressions and interjections

Yáh? — What? (said when repetition of a statement is desired)
Ną. — Here. (said when handing something to someone)
Shá'íí'ąo dá gooyéé. — It is a nice evening.
Shá'íí'ą. — The sun has set.
Tł'é' goslį́í. — Night has come.
Sǫǫs góníí. — There are stars out.
Sǫǫs k'éts'iłii. — The stars are shining.
Hat'é ádzaa? — What happened?
Dá éíná. — That's all, it is finished.
Haéé'ą. — Said when parting, or in agreement.

Doo ásį. — It's all right.
Doo ánsį. — I'm all right.

Cultural note

To the Jicarilla Apaches east is a sacred direction. The doors of the *koghą,* and even the openings of sweat-baths and the gates of corrals face the rising sun. During ceremonials, incantations and prayers are spoken in that direction. And, in past tradition, when a death in the family occurred the camp was moved to the east. The directions, sunwise, or *shák'ehgo* (the sun along its track), are *sháha'áí, shádii'áí, shá'ii'áí* and *náakosii.* Traditionally, when entering a *koghą,* women moved to the left, southward, or *shádii'áí'yéo,* and men to the right, northward, or *náakosii'yéo* to be seated.

A selective comparison of some Apachean terms

When did you go there? I went yesterday.

Jicarilla:	Ha'dą́ dá'kwéé nasínyá? Adą́dą́ naséyá.
Mescalero:	Ha'dą́' áká naa'sínya? Adą́ą́ naa'sííya.
Western:	Haną́' ákú nasínyaa? Adąąną́' nasííyaa.
Navajo:	Hádą́ą́' ákǫ́ǫ́ nisíníyá? Adą́ą́dą́ą́' niséyá.

Unit 10 ◀◀◀◀

Dialog

Iyáná' naméntchii? — What are you buying?
Bíít miijéé'íí naméshchii. — I am buying a car battery.

Nyii'ííshą, iyáná' nayétchii? — How about your son, what is he buying?
Bíít miikee shíí bíít miik'a nayétchii. — He is buying tires and oil.

He é té' naméntchii? — Are you going to buy some clothes?
Ch'at naméshchii. — I am going to buy a hat.

Díí ch'atíí dá'kwíí íílíí? — How much does this hat cost?
Káadin béeso shíí nóóst'ádin sindáo íílíí. — It costs thirty dollars and ninety cents.

Dátánéé íílíí. — It is expensive.
Doo tao íílíí da. — It isn't expensive.

Ná naméshchii. — I'll buy it for you.
He shá naméntchii? Éí nzhǫ. Ihéedń. — You'll buy it for me? That's nice. Thank you.

Vocabulary

1. naméntchii — you buy, are buying
2. bíít miijéé — car battery
3. bíít miijéé'íí — a particular battery
4. naméshchii — I buy, am buying
5. nyii'íí — your son
6. nyii'ííshą — how about your son
7. bíít miikee — tire(s)
8. bíít miik'a — oil
9. nayétchii — he buys, is buying
10. é - clothes, dress
11. te' — some
12. ch'at — hat; díí ch'atíí — this particular hat
13. dá'kwíí — how much
14. íílíí — it costs
15. káadin — thirty
16. béeso — dollar(s)
17. shíí — and
18. nóóst'ádin — ninety
19. sindáo — cent(s)
20. dátánéé — much, many, a lot
21. tao — much, a lot
22. ná — for you
23. shá — for me
24. éí nzhǫ — that's nice
25. ihéedń — thank you

44

Explanations

1. The battery of a car is called *bííł miijéé* (car its heart). The tires are termed *bííł miikee* (car its feet or shoes), and *bííł miik'a* literally means *car its fat.* Such anthropomorphic taxonomy is common in the Apachean languages when referring to the parts of a car, for example, Navajo *chidí bináá'* (car its eyes, i.e., headlights) and Western Apache *nałbiil bibid* (car its stomach, i.e., gas tank). For a fascinating essay on this subject see "Semantic Aspects of Linguistic Acculturation" by Keith Basso, in his *Western Apache Language and Culture: Essays in Linguistic Anthropology,* pp. 15-24, published by the University of Arizona Press, Tucson.

2. The relative enclitic *-íí* is appended to bííł miijéé to render the meaning *the* or *a particular car battery.* It is likewise employed in the question *Díí ch'ałíí dá'kwíí íílíí?* to mean *this particular hat.*

3. *Dáłánéé íílįį* (much it costs) is rendered as *it is expensive,* and *doo łąo íílįį da* as *it is inexpensive.*

4. Note that *naméshchii* can mean *I buy, I am buying,* and may express a future action *I'll buy, I am going to buy.*

5. The postpositions of Apache are used much like prepositions. The expressions *for me, for you, for him* are represented in Jicarilla Apache as *shá, ná, má (yá),* where the preposition *for* is translated as *-á* and is in a post position to the prepositional elements *sh-, n-,* and *m- (y-).* Thus, *shá naméntchii* (buy it for me) or *má naméshchii* (I'll buy it for him, her). Note that when there is a coincidence of 3rd person verb and object *má* changes to *yá: yá nayéłchii* (he, she is buying it for him, her).

Review and practice with new vocabulary

1. He látsínéé łe' naméntchii? — Are you buying some bracelets?
   Dooda, jaatł'ół łe' naméshchii — No, I am buying some earrings.

2. Iyáná' nayéłchii? — What is she buying?
   La'níích'éé łe' nayéłchii. — She is buying some rings.

3. Dá'kwíí íílįį? — How much do they cost?
   Gosts'idin shįį ashdle' béeso íílįį. — They cost seventy-five dollars.

4. Iyáná' naméntchiigo hánt'įį? — What do you want to buy?
   É łe' naméshchiigo hásht'įį. — I want to buy some clothes.

Ké łe' naméshchiigo hásht'íí. — I want to buy some shoes.
Étso naméshchiigo hásht'íí. — I want to buy a coat.
Tł'aazis (buttocks bag) naméshchiigo hásht'íí. — I want to buy pants.

5. He é łe' naméshíńłchii? — Did you buy some clothes?
Aoo, é łe' naméshéłchii. — Yes, I bought a dress.
Sis naméshéłchii. — I bought a belt.
Kézis (foot bag) łe' naméshéłchii. — I bought some socks.
Gamíisa (Spanish, *camisa*) naméshéłchii. — I bought a shirt.

6. He díí látsínéé nayéshchii? — Did she buy this bracelet?
Aoo, énda éí doo miik'eh da. — Yes, but it doesn't fit her.

7. He éí nk'eh? — Does it fit you?
Aoo, éí shiik'eh — Yes, it fits me.

8. Éí látsínéé maa naméshchii. — I'll buy that bracelet from her.
Éí ná naméshchii. — I'll buy it for you.

Note the use of *shaa, naa, maa* in number 8 above, and in 9 and 10 below, to mean *from me, you, him, her.* Contrast tone level and vowel length with *shá, ná, má* (for me, you, him, her).

9. Łíí ha'ń maa nayéshchii? — From whom did he, she buy the horse?
Shaa nayéshchii. — He, she bought it from me.

10. He díí bííł shaa naménłchii? — Are you buying this car from me?
Aoo, naa naméshchii. — Yes, I'll buy it from you.

Note in numbers 11 and 12 below the use of the postpositions *shiich'į, nch'į, miich'į* (to me, to you, to him, her), with the forms of the verb *to buy,* to render the meaning *to sell to*

11. He bóó miich'į naméshíńłchii? — Did you sell the cow to him, her?
Aoo, éí miich'į naméshéłchii. — Yes, I sold it to him, her.

12. He nbíilii shiich'į naménłchii? — Will you sell me your car?
Aoo, éí nch'į naméshchii. — Yes, I'll sell it to you.

13. Iyáná' gó? — What else?
Dá éíná. — That's all.

Comprehension

Kįį'yé déyá. Dáan łe' naméshchii. Iibe' shįį́ gahée naméshchiigo hásht'įį́. Shii'máá má naméshchii. Adádá bííł miikee naméshéłchii. Shiika'éé é łe' nayéshchii. Éí shá nayéshchii. Éí nzhǫ́ nt'éé. Yiskǫ́o shiichóó łįį́ łe' shiich'oonííí yiich'į nayéłchii. Naakii yiskǫ́o (in two days) shiichóó bóó maa naméshchii.

Questions

1. Ha'yénáą deeyá? — Where is he going?
2. Iyáná' nayéłchii? — What is he buying?
3. Ha'ń yá nayéłchii? — For whom is he buying?
4. Adádá iyáná' nayéshchii? — What did he buy yesterday?
5. Miika'éé iyáná' nayéshchii? — What did his father buy?
6. Ha'ń é yá nayéshchii? — For whom did he buy clothes?
7. Yiskǫ́o miichóó iyáná' miich'oonííí yiich'į nayéłchii? — What is his grandmother selling to his friend tomorrow?
8. He miichóó bóó yaa nayéłchii? — Is he going to buy a cow from his grandmother?

More numbers

naadin dáłaa'é:	21	káadin:	30	nóóst'ádin:	90
naadin naakii:	22	díshdin:	40	dáłéediikoo:	100
naadin kái'ii:	23	ashdla'din:	50	naakiidiikoo:	200
		goská'din:	60	mííl:	1,000
(The numbers 24–29		gosts'idin:	70	mííltso:	one million
are formed in the same way)		tseebíídin:	80	biiyóon:	one billion

Expressions

Iyáná' át'é? — What is this, that?
Abáachiik'ehgo "clothes" iyáná' át'é? — What is "clothes" in Apache?
Ashdle' béeso míighahgo. — Five dollars worth.
Dá ma'goołkąą'é. — It is funny.
Doo ma'goołkąą da. — It is not funny.
Dá shił iigoołkąą'é. — I am having fun.
He nł iigoołkąą? — Are you having fun?
Doo yá'ńchédé! — Quiet! Keep quiet! Shut up!

A selective comparison of some Apachean terms

I bought some cattle for her.

Jicarilla: Bóó łe' má naméshéłchii.
Mescalero: Iyáné łii bá nahéłdii'.
Western: Bagashi (magashi; iyání) ła' bá naháłdii' (naháłnii').
Navajo: Béegashii ła' bá naháłnii'.

Note: *Iyání* in Navajo and *iyánéé* in Jicarilla Apache both mean *buffalo*.

Unit 11   ◀◀◀◀

Dialog

He dikosdéé ne'ńłde? — Did you catch cold?
Aoo, dikosdéé she'ńłde. — Yes, I caught cold.
Dinshnii. — I am sick.

Hat'éonáá dikosdéé ne'ńłde? — How did you catch cold?
Tł'ó'yé shee yiiską́. — I spent the night outside.

De'ńljee. — Let's build a fire.
Shíí doo shił ásį, diskos íí yąą. — That's fine, because I have a cough.

He dá nł goosdo? — Are you warming up?
Aoo, dákoo dá shił goosdo. — Yes, I am warming up now.

Vocabulary

1. dikosdéé — a cold
2. she'ńłde — it entered me
3. dinshnii — I am sick, ill
4. hat'éonáá — how, in what way, why
5. ne'ńłde — it entered you
6. tł'ó'yé — outside
7. shee yiiską́ — I spent the night
8. de'ńljee — Let's build a fire
9. shíí — I, as for me
10. doo shił ásį — it is fine with me
11. diskos — I cough, am coughing
12. íí yąą — because, on account of
13. dá nł goosdo — you are warm, warming up
14. dákoo — now
15. dá shił goosdo — I am warm, warming up

Explanations

1. *Dikosdéé* is a cold or a cough.

2. *Ne'ńłde* is comprised of the components *ne'-* (into you) and *-ńłde* (it came, or moved). Thus, literally, *a cold moved into you*. It follows that *she'ńłde* and *me'ńłde*

mean *I caught a cold* and *he, she caught a cold*. Compare with Navajo *shiih yítk'aaz*, where *shiih* signifies *into me* and *yítk'aaz* is translated as *coldness moved*.

3. The stem *-niih* in the expression *dinshniih* conveys the meaning *pain*, therefore *dinshniih* means *I am in pain, I hurt,* and by extension, *I am ill*.

4. The word *tł'ó'yé* (outside, outdoors) is constituted of the element *tł'ó'* (outdoors) and *-yé* (at). *Tł'ó'* must always be used with a place enclitic such as *-yé*

5. The expression *shee yiiską́* (I spent the night) is comprised of *shee* (with me) and *yiiską́* (the passage of night and the beginning of dawn have occured). Translate *you spent the night* and *he, she spent the night* as *nee yiiską́* and *mee yiiską́*. To express the future use the verb *yiiłkáí*. See number 3 in the review and practice below.

6. *Doo shił ásį* carries the literal meaning *with me there is no need or want*, therefore *it is fine with me*.

7. *Nł goosdo* (you are warm, are warming up) is translated literally as *with you it is warm*. Thus *shił goosdo* and *mił goosdo* mean *I am warm* and *he, she is warm*. The idiomatic configuration *-ił goosdo* also means *one is intoxicated*.

Review and practice with new vocabulary

1. Ha'yé nee yiiską́? — Where did you spend the night?
   Shiichóó miigha'yé shee yiiską́. — I spent the night at my mother's house.

2. Nshdázha ha'yé mee yiiską́? — Where did your sister spend the night?
   Éí miigha'yé mee yiiską́. — She spent the night at her house.

3. Díí tł'é'sha, ha'yé nee yiiłkáí? — How about tonight, where will you spend the night?
   Blanco'yé shee yiiłkáí. — I'll spend the night in Blanco.

4. He díńnii? — Are you sick?
   Aoo, dinshnii. — Yes, I am sick.

5. He diinii? — Is he, she sick?
   Éí doo diinii da. — He, she isn't sick.

6. Ha'ną́ą k'e' diinii? — What ails you?
   (The terms *k'e' diinii* and *neesgai* below are interchangeable)

a. Hishdló. — I am cold.
b. Diskos. — I am coughing.
c. Shiitsii k'e' diinii. — My head aches.
d. Shiidáá neesgai. — My eye(s) hurt.
e. Shiichísh neesgai. — My nose hurts.
f. Shiize' k'e' dinii. — My mouth hurts.
g. Shiiwoo k'e' diinii. — My tooth aches.
h. Shiizoł neesgai. — I have a sore throat.
i. Shiijaa k'e' diinii. — I have an earache.
j. Shiijádii neesgai. — My leg hurts.
k. Shiigaan k'e' diinii. — My arm hurts.
l. Shiikee neesgai. — My foot hurts
m. Shiiwos k'e' diinii. — My shoulder hurts.
n. Shiidéé'shíí neesgai. — My back hurts.
o. Shiibii neesgai. — I have a stomach ache.
p. Shiijé' k'e' diinii. — My chest hurts.
q. Shiigwo neesgai. — My knee hurts.

7. He ndló? — Are you cold?
   Aoo, hishdló. — Yes I am cold.

8. He hiidló? — Is he, she cold?
   Doo hiidló da. — He, she is not cold.

9. He mił goosdo? — Is he warm?
   Aoo, mił goosdo. — Yes, he is warm.

10. He bił ńńzįį? — Are you sleepy?
    Aoo, bił nsįį. — Yes, I am sleepy.
    Bił ńzįį. — He, she is sleepy.

11. He dííłkos? — Do you have a cough?
    Dooda, doo diskos da. — No, I don't have a cough.

12. He diłkos? — Does she have a cough?
    Aoo, doo ńdaadé diłkos. — Yes, she is coughing hard.

13. He miizoł neesgai? — Does he have a sore throat?
    Aoo, miizoł k'e' diinii. — Yes, he has a sore throat.

14. Iyáná' yííkát'íí? — What does she want?
    Iloo łe' yííkát'íí. — She wants some ice.

15. Iyáná' gó? — What else?
    Doo mégosį da. — I don't know.
    Ména'íídńłkiih. — Ask her.

16. Gahée dá'kwíí íílįį? — How much is the coffee?
    Ha'dííshą? — Which one?

17. Díí'íí. — This one.
    Ashdle' béeso shį́į́ díshdin sindáo. — Five dollars and forty cents.

16. Ha'yé nghą? — Where is your home?
    Bawóososhį́į́ sháha'áí'yéo shiighą. — My home is east of Pagosa.

17. Nchóó ha'yé miighą? — Where is your grandmother's home?
    Įi'eeshį́į́ náakosii'yéo miighą. — Her home is north of here.

Comprehension

Yiskąo háasbila'yé déyá. Dinishnii. Doo ńdaadé diskos shį́į́ shiizoł neesgai. Shiibii gó k'e' diiniih. Tł'é'dą́ tł'ó'yé shee yiiská áshį́į́ dikosdéé she'ńłde.

Questions

1. Ha'yé deeyá? — Where is he going?
2. Ha'go dá'kwéé deeyá? — When is he going there?
3. He diłkos? — Does he have a cough?
4. He miizoł neesgai? — Does he have a sore throat?
5. He miibii k'e' diiniih? — Does his stomach hurt?
6. He miikee neesgai? — Does his foot hurt?
7. Tł'é'dą́ miighą'yé mee yiiská? — Did he spend the night at home?
8. He dikosdéé me'ńłde? — Did he catch cold?

Expressions

Shóo! — Hey!
Naach'á. — It's a lie.
Naanch'á. — You are lying.
Naach'á. — He, she is lying.
Naashch'á. — I am lying.

Cultural note

The sing (*hada'dii'éí*), or chant, is done to propitiate an offended power or powers who have sent illness. It is traditionally the influence of such powers that is the root of sickness and must be removed by chant, or in the event of epidemics, by both chant and ceremonial dancing. The potency of the chant and its performance by the medicine man, the *haskįįyíí gokaałii* (the man who chants), is more important than specific herbs or medicines used. The cure of disease is closely involved with native religion. Among the Jicarilla sickness was traditionally sent away to the north, or *náakosii'yéo*. The Apachean peoples find no incompatibility in the concomitant use of both modern medicine or medical facilities and the chant.

A selective comparison of some Apachean terms

The coffee is boiled.

Jicarilla:	Gahée shiibéésh.
Mescalero:	Gaxee' shiibésh.
Western:	Túdiłhił (dark water) hishbéézh.
Navajo:	Gohwééh (ahwééh) shibéézh.

Unit 12 ◀◀◀◀

Dialog

Díí ííkiníí ha'yé? — Where does this road go?
Díí ííkiníí Chama'yé. — This is the road to Chama.

Éí ííkiníí kósiłką'yé. — That's the road to the lake.
Éí ííkiníí ík'ą́ą́'yé. — That's the road to the hills.

He ííkiníí goshtł'ish? —- Is the road muddy?
Dooda, doo goshtł'ish da. — No, it's not muddy.

Ííkin hat'é ásį? — How is the road?
Ííkin doo ásį. — The road is all right.

Ííkin séí. — The road is sandy.
Ííkin nzhǫ́. — The road is good.

Ha'yéną́ą Haskiiyíí Vigil miighą? — Where is Mr. Vigil's home?
Ndééch'į miighą. — His home is over there.

Vocabulary

1. díí — this
2. éí — that
3. ííkin — road
4. díí ííkiníí — this particular road
5. ha'yé — where to
6. kósiłką — lake
7. ík'ą́ą́' — hill(s)
8. he — question indicator
9. goshtł'ish — mud, muddy
10. hat'é — how, in what condition
11. doo ásį — all right, o.k.
12. séí — sandy
13. nzhǫ́ — it is good
14. haskiiyíí — man, husband, Mr.
15. ndééch'į — over there

Explanations

1. The word *ííkin* (road) is followed here by the relative enclitic *-íí*, an element that was discussed in Unit 10 (Explanations, number 2). Used here with *díí* (this) it may be rendered as *this particular road*. Further discussion of the enclitic appears in Unit 16. Compare the noun with Mescalero *íntine*, Western Apache *intin* or *itin*, and Navajo *atiin*.

2. Remember that *ha'yé* can mean both *to where* and *at where*.

3. The word *kósiłká* (lake) is constituted of *kó(h)* (water) and *siłká* (it is in position), the stem of which, *-ká*, defines a liquid in an open depression or bowl, hence *lake*.

4. *Ík'áá'* (hills, mountains) is also spoken as *hík'áá'*.

5. *Goshtł'ish* means *mud* as well as *muddy*.

6. *Séí* translates as both *sandy* and *sand*.

7. *Doo ásį* conveys the idiomatic meaning *all right, pretty good*.

8. The word *ndééch'į* (over there) is comprised of *ndéé* (there) and *-ch'į* (in the direction of), thus literally *there in that direction*.

Review and practice with new vocabulary

1. He ííkin séí? — Is the road sandy?
   Dooda, ííkin tsé. — No, the road is rocky.

2. He ííkin nzhǫ́? — Is the road good?
   Dooda, ííkin godiwoł. — No, the road is bumpy.

3. Ííkin hat'é ásį? — What is the condition of the road?
   Ííkin godiłkǫǫh. — The road is smooth.

4. Díí ííkiníí ha'yé? — Where does this road go?
   Díí ííkiníí kįį'yé. — This road goes to town (to the store(s)).

5. Éí ííkiníísha? — How about that road?
   Éí ííkiníí Abáachii miikéyaa'yé. — That's the road to the Apache reservation.

6. N'máá ha'yé miighą? — Where is your mother's home?
   Ndééch'į miighą. — Her home is over there.

7. Ntsóóyéé ha'yé miighą? — Where is your grandfather's home?
   Įį'eeshį́į́ shádii'áí'yéo miighą. — His home is south of here.

8. Ha'go ą́'ee na'iizii? — When do you work there?
   Jį́į́go ą́'ee na'iisii. — I work there during the day.
   Tł'é'go ą́'ee na'iisii. — I work there at night.
   Dá'łaaná ą́'ee na'iisii. — I work there all the time.
   Dąągo ą́'ee na'iisii. — I work there in the spring.
   Shį́į́go ą́'ee na'iisii. — I work there in the summer.
   Dą́ą́k'eego ą́'ee na'iisii. — I work there in the fall.
   Haigo ą́'ee na'iisii. — I work there in the winter.

9. He dikosdéé me'ńłde? — Did she catch cold?
   Aoo, doo ńdaadé diłkos. — Yes, she is really coughing.

10. Dííshą? — How about you?
    Doo she'ńłde da. — I didn't catch a cold.

11. Iyáná'ííká éí diiniih? — Why is he sick?
    Tł'ó'yé mee yiiská̧. — He spent the night outside.

12. He tł'ó'yé nee yiiská̧? — Did you spend the night outside?
    Aoo, dził miikáá'yé. — Yes, on the mountain.

13. He dá goosk'as'é ńt'éé? — Was it very cold?
    Doo ńdaadé goosk'as ńt'éé. — It was terribly cold.

14. He de'dínłjéé? — Did you build a fire?
    Aoo, de'dééłjéé. — Yes, I built a fire.
    Chish góníí ńt'éé. — There was firewood.

15. He nyii'į́į́ de'ńłjéé? — Did your son build a fire?
    Dooda, chish édįį. — No, there was no firewood.

16. Ha'yé nghą? — Where is your home?
    Įį'eeshį́į́ doo aada da. — Not far from here.

17. Nzhǫ́go nandágo. — Take care of yourself (walk about carefully).
    Aoo, díí gó ąą. — Yes, you too.

56

Comprehension

Díí ííkiníí dziłyé. Éí doo goshtł'ish da. Ííkin tsé shį́į́ godiwoł. Shiichóó miigha'yé déyá. Dził miikáá'yé miigha. Naakii yiskā́dā́ tł'ó'yé shee yiiská dził miikáá'yé. Dá goosk'as'é ńt'éé shį́į́ de'déétjéé.

Questions

1. Díí ííkin ha'yé? — Where does this road go?
2. He éí goshtł'ish? — Is it muddy?
3. Ííkiníí hat'é ásį? — How is the road?
4. Ha'yé deeyá? — Where is he, she going?
5. Miichóó ha'yé miigha? — Where is his grandmother's home?
6. Ha'dā́ tł'ó'yé mee yiiskā́? — When did he spend the night outside?
7. Ha'yé tł'ó'yé mee yiiskā́? — Where did he spend the night outside?
8. Iyáná'ííká de'ńtjéé? — Why did he build a fire?

Adjectives

Káził ńdlii. — The stew is burned.
Itsį̇́į ńłdzii. — The meat is spoiled.
Kółbáíí ńk'ǫsh. — The tiswin is bitter.
Díí itsį̇́į dá diits'idé. — This meat is really tough.
Lósii dá łika'é. — The candy is sweet.
Iibe' ńk'ǫǫsh. — The milk is sour.

Expressions

Ádńíí. — You are kidding.
Gé ntǫ́ǫ́'é. — It is ridiculous.
Doo nzhǫ́ da. — It is no good.

A selective comparison of some Apachean terms

This meat is tough.

Jicarilla:	Díí itsį̇́į diits'id.	Western:	Díí itsį' dits'ag.
Mescalero:	Díí itsį diits'a.	Navajo:	Díí atsį' dits'id.

Unit 13 ◀◀◀◀

Dialog

Iyáná' híí'íí? — What do you see?
Shǫǫdii (sitł'idéen) hish'íí. — I see a coyote.

Gah hish'íí. — I see a rabbit.
Dzées hish'íí. — I see an elk.
Bįį hish'íí. — I see a deer.
Gwii' bitséégháléé hish'íí. — I see a rattlesnake.

Éíshą, iyáná' yaa'íí? — What about her, what does she see?
Dibé dził yaa'íí. — She sees mountain sheep.

Dlǫ́' yaa'íí. — She sees a prairie dog.
Itsá yaa'íí. — She sees an eagle.
Itséłtsoíí yaa'íí. — She sees a hawk.
Shash yaa'íí. — She sees a bear.

Ha'yé híí'íí? — Where do you see it?
Ndé'ee, chóshch'ilii miiyaayé. — Over there, under the oak tree.

Ndé'ee, tsé miikáá'yé. — Over there, on the rock.
Ndé'ee, ts'e miika'yé. — Over there, among the sagebrush.
Ndé'ee, it'ą́ązháá miiyaayé. — Over there, under the aspen tree.
Ndé'ee, nóoshchii miibąąch'į. — Over there, by the pine tree.
Hayaach'į. — Down there.
Dágich'į. — Up there.

Vocabulary

1. iyáná' — what
2. híí'íí — you see it
3. shǫǫdii (sitł'idéen) — coyote(s)
4. hish'íí — I see it
5. gah — rabbit(s)
6. dzées — elk
7. bįį — deer
8. gwii' bitséégháléé — rattlesnake(s)
9. éíshą — what about him, her
10. yaa'íí — he, she sees it

11. dibé dził — mountain sheep
12. dlǫ' — prairie dog(s)
13. itsá — eagle(s)
14. itséłtsoíí — hawk(s)
15. shash — bear(s)
16. ndé'ee — there, over there
17. chóshch'ilii — oak tree(s)
18. miiyaayé — under it
19. tsé — rock(s)

20. miikáá'yé — on it, on top of it
21. ts'e — sagebrush
22. miika'yé — among it
23. it'ą́ązháá — aspen tree(s)
24. nóoshchii — pine tree(s)
25. miibąąch'į — by it
26. hayaach'į — down there
27. dágich'į — up there

Explanations

1. *Shǫǫdii* (coyote) is also called *sitł'idéen* by the Jicarilla Apaches.

2. The term *gwii' bitséégháléé* (rattlesnake) is literally *snake its tail is a rattle*. Compare with Mescalero *gú bitsee ghátí,* and Western Apache *tł'iish bitseghál.* The Navajos call the rattlesnake *tł'iish ánínígíí* (the snake that talks).

3. The word *itséłtsoíí* (hawk) is comprised of *itsá* (eagle) and *łtsoíí* (the one that is yellow), thus *yellow eagle.*

4. Notice the difference between *tsé* (rock, stone) and *ts'e* (sagebrush), wherein the latter is differentiated from the former by a tone and by a glottal stop, *ts'* versus *ts.* Jicarilla *ts'e* is interestingly close to Navajo *ts'ah.*

5. Compare in vowel length and tone the words *miikáá'yé* (on top of it) and *miika'yé* (among them).

6. *Tsé miikáá'yé* translates literally as *rock it upon at* and *ts'e miika'yé* as *sagebrush it among at.* Contrast these positions with Navajo *tsé bikáa'di* and *ts'ah bitahdi.*

7. Since there are very few plural forms in Jicarilla Apache, the above-named animals, birds and trees may be used to signify either singular or plural. The flora and fauna displayed here are typical of Jicarilla Apache country.

Review and practice with new vocabulary

1. Iyáná' yaa'íí? — What does he see?
   Shǫǫdii łe' yaa'íí. — He sees some coyotes.

59

2. Iyáná' híí'íí? — What do you see?
   Ǫ́ǫ́haiyee łe' hish'íí. I see some chickens.

3. Ha'yé? — Where?
   Éí nóoshzhaa miiyaayé. — Under that spruce tree.

4. He éí nał'eełéé híí'íí? — Do you see those ducks?
   Doo éí hish'íí da. — I don't see them.

5. He éí tsidéé híí'íí? — Do you see that bird?
   Aoo, éí hish'íí. — Yes, I see it.

6. He éí nígotł'its'íí híí'íí? — Do you see that pig?
   Aoo, ndééch'į chish miibąąch'į. — Yes, over there by the tree.

7. Kéesda'yé ha'ń hiinłtsą́? — Whom did you see at the feast?
   Shiitsóóyéé heełtsą́. — I saw my grandfather.

8. Kóńłíí'yé ha'ń yiiłtsą́? — Whom did he see at the river?
   Shiizeedń yiiłtsą́. — He saw my cousin.

9. He nshdázha hiiłtsą́? — Is your sister expecting?
   Aoo, éí hiiłtsą́. — Yes, she's pregnant.

10. Bįį łe' hiinłtsą́? — Did you see some deer?
    Dooda, bįį łe' doo heełtsą́ da. — No, I didn't see any deer.

11. Abáachii miizaa mee yánłkii? — Do you speak Apache?
    Aoo, mee yáshkii. — Yes, I speak it.

    Note above the use of *mee* (by means of it) *yáshkii*, an alternative to *k'eh* (in the manner of) *yáshkii*.

12. He nyii'íí yee yáłkii? — Does your son speak it?
    Aoo, áłts'íísdéo yee yáłkii. — Yes, he speaks it a little.

13. He doo ńdaadégo ánł'íí? — Are you trying hard?
    Aoo, doo ńdaadégo ásh'íí. — Yes, I am trying hard.

14. Éí naakii diidé ha'yé íí'ash? — Where did those two men go?
    Kįį'yé íí'ash. — They went to town.

15. Iyáná'iíká dá'kwéé íí'ásh? — Why did they go there?
    Bííł nayéłchiigo íí yąą. — For the purpose of buying a car.

16. Ha'ń yá na'iizii? — For whom is she working?
    Shá na'iizii. — She is working for me.

17. He ná nayéshchii? — Did he buy it for you?
    Dooda, yá nayéshchii. — No he bought it for him, her.

Comprehension

Adádá dziłyé naséyá. Á'ee bįį shíí shash heełtsą. Shiizeedń gó dá'kwéé naasyá. Áń (he, she) gwii' yiiłtsá. Díijíí (today) kósiłką'yé shǫǫdii łe' hish'íí ndééch'į nóoshchii miiyaayé.

Questions

1. Ha'yé naasyá? — Where did she go?
2. Ha'dą dá'kwéé naasyá? — When did she go there?
3. Á'ee iyáná' yiiłtsą? — What did she see there?
4. He miizeedń dá'kwéé naasyá? — Did her cousin go there?
5. Iyáná' ą'ee yiiłtsą? — What did he see there?
6. Díijíí iyáná' yaa'íí? — What does she see today?
7. Ha'yé éí yaa'íí? — Where does she see them?
8. He éí kósiłką'yé yaa'íí? — Does she see them at the lake?
9. He éí nóoshchii miiyaayé yaa'íí? — Does she see them under a pine tree?

The enclitic -go

You have become acquainted with enclitics such as -yé (direction toward, location), -shíí (from), -dą (past time), and others. The enclitic -go, which you have also seen in earlier units, is a participializer of verbs and an adverbializer of nouns and particles. It is roughly translatable as *while, as, when, as soon as, -ing* (as in *eating*), and *-ly* (as in *cheerfully*).

Practice the following examples:

Na'iisiigo dá shił hooyéé. — I like working.
Méoniisįįgo dá shił hooyéé. — I like learning it.
Isgwéela'yé náshdééhgo doo shił hooyéé da. — I don't like going to school.
K'eh yáshkiigo dá ch'éh ásh'íí. — Speaking it is difficult for me.

61

Á'ee naashágo éí naméshchii. — When I am there (walking about there) I'll buy it.
É łe' hásht'íígo kįį'yé naséyá. — Wanting some clothes I went to the store.
Inłt'ánéé dá hooyéégo k'eh yánłkii. — You speak Navajo well (nicely).
Dá hooyéégo na'iizii. — He works well.
Shíígo (haigo) dá'kwéé déyá. — I'll go there when it is summer (winter).
Doo ńdaadé ásh'íígo méoniisįį. — When I try hard I learn.

Imperatives

Dín'íí! — Look!
Ídlą́! — Drink! (to one person)
Adlą́! — Drink! (to two)
Da'adlą́! — Drink! (to more than two)
Íyą́! — Eat! (to one)
Asą́! — Eat! (to two)
Da'asą́! — Eat! (to more than two)

Adjectives

Łįį́ łibá. — The horse is gray.
Gáagee łizhįį. — A crow is black.
Chíníí łizhįį shį́į́ łigai. — The dog is black and white.
Gwii' łichíí shį́į́ łitso. — The snake is red and yellow.
Tsidéé daatł'ish. — The bird is blue (green).
Bóó dinishzhį. — The cow is brown.
Mósha miitsii dáłánéé. — The cat is hairy.

See note about *łįį́* on page 23.

Cultural note

The Apachean peoples traditionally used animals for religious purposes as well as for food and clothing. Quivers made of skins and feathered arrows were employed in warfare. The bones of birds and animal legs were brought into service during sings and chants. Animals and birds were therefore vital in traditional Apachean ritual and ceremony. The various species of bear, for example, are said to come from the parts of mythical beings. And the skins of certain animals have been widely used as ritualistic and ceremonial appurtenances, while owls, rabbits and the coyote have been prominent in legends and folklore.

A selective comparison of some Apachean terms

I see a jackrabbit.

Jicarilla: Gahtso hish'íí.
Mescalero: Gahtsu da'ush'íí.
Western: Gahcho hish'íí.
Navajo: Gahtsoh yish'í.

Unit 14   ◀◀◀◀

The following material is designed to give you practice in saying *give* or *hand x to me, to him, to her.* The information deals with the changing stem of the handling verb. The stem (the last element of the verb) defines, in an abstract sense, the shape, quality, or size of the object handled. It changes form in pursuit of the definition or explanation of differently shaped or qualified objects.

The verb stem -'ai refers to the handling (in the examples below, *giving*) of a single, bulky, roundish or squarish, often hard object. The stem -'ai is in the imperfective mode (present tense). The stem -'ei is also used alternatively in Jicarilla Apache.

Łeet'áan sha ń'ai. — Give me the bread (loaf).
Bésh sha ń'ai. — Give me the knife.
Ísee sha ń'ai. — Give me the pot.
Itsįį sha ń'ai. — Give me the meat.
Naałtsoozii sha ń'ai. — Give me the book.

The imperfective stem -kai is used to designate the handling of something in an open container, in the examples below, liquids.

Gahée sha ńkai. — Give me the coffee.
Bííł miik'a sha ńkai. — Give me the oil.
Iibe' sha ńkai. — Give me the milk.
Káził sha ńkai. — Give me the stew.
Kólichíí'íí sha ńkai. — Give me the soda pop.

Use the stem that applies to each object given below:

Bííł miik'a…	Naałtsoozii…
Bésh…	Kólichíí'íí…
Łeet'áan..	Itsįį…
Kóh…	Káził…
Ísee…	Iibe'…

Practice until the use of these forms becomes familiar. Many more handling verb stems will be given in the units to follow.

Note below how subject and indirect object may be manipulated:

Ísee sha ń'ai. — Give me the pot.
Ísee na nsh'ai. — I am giving you the pot.

Kóh sha ńkai. — Give me the water.
Kóh na nshkai. — I am giving you the water.

Dialog

He íyą́? — Are you eating?
Aoo, ishą́. — Yes, I am eating.

Iyáná' nyą́? — What are you eating?
Itsįį hishą́. — I am eating meat.

Łe' sha ń'ai. — Give me some.
Aoo, na nsh'ai. — All right, I'll give you some (I'm giving you some).
Ną. — Here you are.

He íinyą́? — Did you eat?
Aoo, ééyą́. — Yes, I ate.

He ídlą́? — Are you drinking?
Aoo, ishdlą́. — Yes, I am drinking.

Iyáná' ndlą́? — What are you drinking?
Gahée hishdlą́. — I am drinking coffee.

Łe' sha ńkai. — Give me some.
Aoo, łe' na nshkai. — Yes, I'll give you some.
Ną. — Here you are.

Ihéedń. He íińdlą́? — Thanks. Did you drink?
Aoo, éédlą́. — Yes, I drank.

Vocabulary

1. he — question indicator
2. íyá — you are eating
3. ishá — I am eating
4. nyá — you are eating (it, something)
5. hishá — I am eating (it, something)
6. íinyá — you ate
7. ééyá — I ate
8. ídlá — you are drinking
9. ishdlá — I am drinking
10. ndlá — you are drinking (it, something)
11. hishdlá — I am drinking (it, something)
12. ííndlá — you drank
13. éédlá — I drank

Explanations

1. *Íyá* means *you are eating,* no direct object expressed. When a direct object is involved in the eating, the verb changes, in this case in the 2nd person singular, to accommodate the object. *Iyáná'* (what) is the direct object in the first example in the above dialog, therefore the verb changes from *íyá* to *nyá* (what are you eating). In the answer to the question the object is *itsįį,* thus the verb changes from *ishá* (I am eating) to *hishá* (I am eating it, i.e., meat).

2. Explanation number 1 above pertains also to all of the verb forms of *ishdlá* (I am drinking). If a direct object is involved the form must be *hishdlá* (I am drinking it). Compare Jicarilla *ishá, hishá, ishdlá, hishdlá* with Navajo *ashá, yishá, ashdlá, yishdlá* and Western Apache *ishąą, hishąą, ishdląą, hishdląą.*

3. In the expression *itsįį łe' sha ń'ai* (give me some meat) the word *sha* signifies *to me.* Syllabic *ń* signifies *you* (singular), and the verb stem *-'ai* (handle, give it) represents the bulky or chunky object *itsįį* (meat).

4. In a phrase such as *kóh sha ńkai* (give me the water), *sha* means *to me.* Syllabic *ń* signifies *you,* and the verbal stem *-kai* expresses the handling of something in an open container, in this case water. If the water were in a closed container the stem *-'ai* would be used.

5. These verb stems may also be used to express the idea *bring it to me.*

Review and practice with new vocabulary

1. He nyii'íí iyą́? — Is your son eating?
   Aoo, iyą́. — Yes, he is eating.

2. Iyáná' yiyą́? — What is he eating?
   Łeet'áan yiyą́. — He is eating bread.

3. N'máá łe' ma ń'ai. — Give some to your mother.
   Aoo, łe' ma nsh'ai. — Yes, I am giving her some.

4. He łe' ya yíí'ai? — Is he giving her some?
   Aoo, łe' ya yíí'ai. — Yes, he is giving her some.

5. He nzhách'į'íí idlą́? — Is your daughter drinking?
   Aoo, idlą́. — Yes, she is drinking.

6. Iyáná' yidlą́? — What is she drinking?
   Iibe' yidlą́. — She is drinking milk.

7. Ndą'ą́ą́ łe' ma ńkai. — Give some to your uncle.
   Aoo, łe' ma nshkai. — Yes, I am giving him some.

8. He łe' ya yíkai? — Is she giving him some?
   Aoo, łe' ya yíkai. — Yes, he is giving her some.

9. He káził nł łiką? — Do you like stew (is it sweet with you?)?
   Aoo, éí hishą́go dá shił hooyéé. — Yes, I like eating it.

10. He tł'ó'yé goosk'asgo dá nł hooyéé? — Do you like cold weather?
    Tł'ó'yé goosdogo dá shił hooyéé. — I like warm weather.

11. Adą́dą́ ha'yéną́ą na'íízii ńt'éé? — Where did you work yesterday?
    Kįį'yé na'iisii ńt'éé. — I was working in town.

12. Kįį'yé naaskaigo ha'ń daayiiłtsą́? — Whom did they see when they went to town?
    Mii'máá daayiiłtsą́. — They saw his mother.

13. He éí ch'ałdéé híí'íí? — Do you see that frog?
    Aoo, ndééch'į chóshch'ilii miide'yé hish'íí. — Yes, I see it over there behind the oak tree.

Comprehension

Itsįį naméshéłchii. Dákoo éí hishą́. Shii'máá gó iyą́. Káził yiyą́. Éí mił liką'é. Shii'máá káził łe' sha yíkai. Áshį́į́ shíí shii'máá itsįį łe' ma nsh'ai.

Questions

1. Iyáná' nayéshchii? — What did she buy?
2. He itsįį yiyą́? — Is she eating the meat?
3. Mii'máá iyáná' yiyą́? — What is her mother eating?
4. He mii'máá káził dá mił liką'é? — Does her mother like stew?
5. Shii'máá iyáná' ya yíkai? — What does her mother give her?
6. Iyáná' miizhách'í'į́í mii'máá ya yíkai? — What does the daughter give to her mother?

Imperatives

Kwe' ńkįį. — Open the door.
Ną́'hęę ńkįį. — Close the door.

A selective comparison of some Apachean terms

Give him the apple.

Jicarilla:	Mansáana ma ń'ai.
Mescalero:	Mansáana ba ń'aa
Western:	Masáana baa ní'aah
Navajo:	Bilasáana baa ní'aah

Unit 15 ◀◀◀◀

Dialog

Iyáná' há nańká? — What are you looking for?
Shiimósha há nanshká. — I am looking for my cat.

He náhiinłtsą́? — Did you find it?
Aoo, náheełtsą́. — Yes, I found it

Iyáná' yííká nanká? — What is she looking for?
Miichíníí yííká nanká. — She is looking for her dog.

He náyiiłtsą́? — Did she find it?
Aoo, náyiiłtsą́. — Yes, she found it.

Nmósha dá'kwíí meeshį́į́? — How old is your cat?
Shiimósha ashdle' meeshį́į́. — My cat is five years old.

Miichíníí dá'kwíí meeshį́į́? — How old is her dog?
Éí naakii meeshį́į́. — He is two years old.

Vocabulary

1. há — for it
2. nańká — you look, you seek
3. shiimósha — my cat
4. nanshká — I look, I seek
5. yííká — for it (3rd person)
6. nanká — he, she seeks
7. miichíníí — his, her dog
8. náyiiłtsą́ — he, she found him, her, it
9. dá'kwíí — how much, how many
10. meeshį́į́ — his, her, its age

Explanations

1. High-toned *há* means *for* or *after* in the sense of *looking for* or *going after*. The 3rd person form of *há* is *yííká*.

2. *Náyiiłtsá* (he, she found her, him, it) consists of the element *ná-,* which means *again,* and *yiiłtsá,* the 3rd person singular verb meaning *he, she saw him, her, it.* A literal rendering of *náyiiłtsá* is *he saw him again,* that is, *he found him.*

3. *Meeshį́į́* (his, her age) is comprised of the postposition *mee* (with him, her, it) and the noun *shį́į́* (summer). Hence, a literal rendering of *ashdle' meeshį́į́* (he is five years old) would be *five with him summers.* It is of interest to note that the Navajo phrase *ashdla' binááhai* literally translates as *five his repeated winters.*

Review and practice with new vocabulary

1. He mek'e'iilchíí há nańká? — Are you looking for a pencil?
   Me'iichíshíí há nanshká. — I'm looking for the crayon(s).

2. He me'iik'aashíí yííká nanká? — Is he looking for the saw?
   Mená'iigodíí yííká nanká. — He is looking for the hoe.

3. He mets'iiłt'eesíí há nańká? — Are you looking for the frying pan?
   Begozhǫ́'íí há nanshká. — I'm looking for the broom.

4. He ńna'ą́ą́ há nańká? — Are you looking for your older brother?
   Aoo, éí há nanshká. — Yes, I am looking for him.

5. He éí náhiinłtsą́? — Did you find him?
   Aoo, náheełtsą́. — Yes, I found him.

6. He miida'ą́ą́ náyiiłtsą́? — Did he find his uncle?
   Aoo, náyiiłtsą́. — Yes, he found him.

7. He goskáan meeshį́į́? — Is she six years old?
   Gosts'idii meeshį́į́ — She is seven years old.

8. He ashdla'din neeshį́í? — Are you fifty years old?
   Ashdla'din naakii sheeshį́í. — I am fifty two years old.

9. Dá'kwíí neeshį́í? — How old are you?
   Díshdin sheeshį́í. — I am forty years old.

10. Ǫǫzhazhį́į́ dá'kwíí meeshį́í? — How old is the baby?
    Ǫǫzhazhį́į́ gonesnáan meeńdeezii. — The baby is ten months old.
    Éí kái'ii meeńdeezii. — It is three months old.

11. He nhaskįįyíí wées nilįį? — Is your husband a judge?
    Ółkai'íí nilįį. — He is a student.

12. He ndádéé na'iizii? — Does your older sister work?
    Ła'go na'iizii. — Sometimes she works.
    Na'iiziigo dá mił hooyéé. — She likes working.

13. He mii'á isgwéela nádééh? — Does his wife go to school?
    Shįįgo isgwéela nádééh. — She goes to school in the summer.

14. He isgwéela nádééhgo éí dá mił hooyéé? — Does she like going to school?
    Aoo, dá mił hooyéé. — Yes, she likes it.

15. Ishágo shił hooyéé, dííshą? — I like to eat, how about you?
    Ashágo dá shił hooyéé. — I really like to eat.

16. Łeet'áan sha ń'ai. — Hand me the bread.
    Haéé'ą, na nsh'ai. — Yes, I'll hand it to you.

17. He ídlágo dá nł hooyéé? — Do you like to drink?
    Aoo, ishdlágo dá shił hooyéé. — Yes, I like to drink.

18. Kółbáíí ma ńkai. — Hand him the tiswin.
    Haéé'ą, ma nshkai. — All right, I'll hand it to him.

19. Iyáná' nyą? — What are you eating?
    Itsįį hishą. — I am eating meat.
    Éí gó itsįį yiyą. — She's also eating meat.

20. Iyáná' ndlą? — What are you drinking?
    Gahée hishdlą. — I am drinking coffee.
    Éí gó gahée yidlą. — He's also drinking coffee.

21. Iyáná'ííká miich'į yánłkii? — Why are you talking to her?
    Miich'į yáshkiigo dá shił hooyéé. — I like talking to her.

22. Abáachii k'ehgo shiich'į yánłkii. — Speak to me in Apache.
    Aoo, Abáachii k'ehgo nch'į yáshkii. — Yes, I'll talk to you in Apache.

23. Iyáná'ííká ą́'ee na'íízii? — Why are you working there?
    Dá shił hooyéé ééká. — Because I like it.

24. Iyáná'iíka gahée doo ndlá da? — Why don't you drink the coffee?
    Doo shił łiką da ééká. — Because I don't like it.

Comprehension

Shiichíníí há nanshká ńt'éé adádá. Kįį'yé náheełtsá. Shiichíníí naakii meeshíí.
Éí Abáachii k'ehgo miich'į yáshkii. Abáachii k'ehgo miich'į yáshkiigo éí yidiits'e.

Questions

1. Adádá iyáná' yiíká nanká ńt'éé? — What was he looking for yesterday?
2. Ha'yé náyiiłtsá? — Where did he find it?
3. Miichíníí dá'kwíí meeshíí? — How old is his dog?
4. He Mągáanii k'ehgo yiich'į yáłkii? — Does he speak to him in English?
5. He miichíníí yidiits'e? — Does his dog understand?

A new handling verb

The imperfective stem -łkee refers to the handling of an animate object:

Mósha sha ńłkee. — Give me the cat.
Ǫǫzhazhíí sha ńłkee. — Hand me the baby.
Dibé miizháá sha ńłkee. — Hand me the lamb.

Use the appropriate stem:

Kóh…   Ch'ałdéé…
Bésh…   Łeet'áan
Tsidéé…   Chíníí…
Káził…

Personal characteristics

Ma ch'óolíí. — He, she is reliable.
Doo ma ch'óolíí da. — He, she is unreliable.
Míínii dá nzhǫ. — Her mind is very good.

72

Dá góyą'é. — She is very intelligent.

Doo góyą. — He is stupid.

Dá mił góóyé'é. — She is lazy.

Yá ńzįį. — She is shy.

Yá nsįį. — I am shy.

He yá ńnzįį? — Are you shy?

Emotions and dispositions

Shił gózhǫ́. — I am happy (with me it is beautiful).

Mił goosdo. — He, he is drunk (also, warm).

Mił gohwii. — He is content.

Shił gótǫ́ǫ́'é. — I am sad, melancholy.

Mił éégózįį. — He, she is learned, knowledgeable.

Mee nésdzii. — I am afraid of it.

Yee néłdzii. — He, she is afraid of it.

He mee nénłdzii? — Are you afraid of it?

A selective comparison of Apachean terms

My wife is knowledgeable.

Jicarilla — Shii'á (shii'iisdzáníí) mił éégózįį

Mescalero — Shighaasdzą' égúsį

Western — Shi'aad bił ígózįį.

Navajo — She'esdzą́ą́ bił ééhózin.

Unit 16 ◀◀◀◀

Dialog

Ha'yéną̄ą nandá ńt'éé? — Where have you been?
Inłt'ánéé miikéyaa'yé naashá ńt'éé — I have been on the Navajo reservation.

Ha'dą́ nańndzá? — When did you return?
Adą́dą́ nánsdzá? — I got back yesterday.

Ha'go shiich'į ná'ńlé? — When are you going to pay me?
Yiską́o nch'į ná'nshłé. — I'll pay you tomorrow.

N'máá miich'į ná'ńnlá? — Did you pay your mother?
Aoo, miich'į ná'nílá. — Yes, I paid her.

He nshdázha yiich'į ná'íílé? — Is your sister paying her?
Yiich'į ná'íílá. — She paid her.

Vocabulary

1. kéyaa — land, country
2. Inłt'ánéé miikéyaa — Navajo reservation
3. ha'dą́ — when
4. nańndzá — you returned
5. adą́dą́ — yesterday
6. nánsdzá — I returned
7. shiich'į — to me
8. ná'ńlé — you pay, will pay
9. nch'į — to you
10. ná'nshłé — I pay, will pay
11. miich'į — to her
12. ná'ńnlá — you paid
13. ná'nílá — I paid
14. ná'íílé — he pays, will pay
15. ná'íílá — he paid

Explanations

1. The verbs *naashá, nandá, naaghá* signify *walking about*. The common phrase for *he, she is in Dulce* is *Lósii'yé naaghá* (he, she is walking about in Dulce). The use of the past tense marker *ńt'éé* puts the phrase into an imperfect past, *Lósii'yé naaghá ńt'éé* (he, she was in Dulce).

2. *Ná'nílá* (I paid), as well as the other forms of this verb presented above, is in the perfective mode, equivalent to a past tense, action completed.

3. *Shiich'į* consists of the indirect object pronoun *shii-* (me) and the postposition *-ch'į* (to, toward). The phrase *shiich'į ná'nlé* (pay me) is rendered literally as *me to(ward) you pay*.

Review and practice with new vocabulary

1. Nhaskįį'yíí ha'yé naaghá ńt'éé? — Where has your husband been?
   Dziłntsaa'yé naaghá ńt'éé. — He has been in Albuquerque.

2. Ha'dą́ nádzá? —When did he return?
   Ashdle' yiskádą́ nádzá. — He got back five days ago.

3. He Chama'yé dínyá? — Are you going to Chama?
   Aoo, dá'kwéé déyá. — Yes, I'm going there.

4. Ha'go nádńdáát? — When will you return?
   Yiskáo nádiishdáát. — I'll return tomorrow.

5. Áń ha'go nádaadáát? — When will he return?
   Naakii yiskáo nádaadáát. — He'll return in two days.

6. Ha'go sha nádńdáát? — When are you coming back to see me?
   Dák'adéé na nádiishdáát. — I'll return soon to see you.

7. Sha nádńdáát. — Come back to see me.
   Aoo, na nádiishdáát. — I'll be back to see you.

8. Dák'adéé shiich'į ná'nlé. — Pay me soon.
   Dákoo nch'į ná'nshłé. — I'll pay you now.

9. Dá'kwíí zháał miich'į ná'ńnlá? — How much money did you pay her?
   Ashdle' béeso miich'į ná'nílá. — I paid her five dollars.

10. He miich'į ná'ńlé? — Are you going to pay him?
    Doo miich'į ná'nshłé da. — I'm not going to pay him.

11. Iyáná' há nańká? — What are you looking for?
    Shiilį́į' há nanshká. — I am looking for my horse.

75

12. He náhiinłtsą? — Did you find it?
    Dooda, doo náheełtsá da. — No, I didn't find it.

Comprehension

Abáachii miikéyaa'yé naashá ńt'éé. Adądą́ nánsdzá. Shiizeedń Lósii'yé naaghá ńt'éé. Kái'ii yiską́dą́ nádzá. Díshdin meeshį́į́. Yiską́o ma nádiishdáá. Gonesnáan béeso miich'į ná'nshłé.

Questions

1. Ha'yé naaghá ńt'éé? — Where has she been?
2. Ha'dą́ nádzá? — When did she return?
3. Miizeedń ha'yé naaghá ńt'éé? — Where has her cousin been?
4. Dá'kwíí meeshį́į́? — How old is he (she)?
5. Ha'go ya nádaadáá? — When is she going back to see him?
6. Dá'kwíí zháał yiich'į ná'íílé? — How much money will he pay her?

The enclitic -íí

This enclitic means *the one who*, or *this, that, those particular one(s)*.

Áń ndé'ee dah sidá. — He, she is sitting over there.
Áń ndé'ee dah sidá'íí. — He, she is the one sitting over there.

Áń Lósii'yé naaghá. — He, she is in Dulce.
Áń Lósii'yé naaghá'íí. — He, she is the one in Dulce.

Dáan naméshchii. — I am buying food.
Dáan naméshchii'íí. — I am the one buying food.

Áń míízhii Joe. — His name is Joe.
Áń míízhii Joe'íí. — He is the one named Joe.

Áń idlą́. — He drinks.
Áń idlą́'íí. — He is the one who drinks (drunkard).

Note the use of this enclitic in other adjectival forms:

Łį́į́ łibá. — The horse is gray.   Łį́į́ łibá'íí — The gray horse
Gáagee łizhį́į. — The crow is black.   Gáagee łizhį́į'íí — The black crow
Mósha dinishzhį. — The cat is brown.   Mósha dinishzhį'íí — The brown cat

More weather terms

Tł'ó'yé hat'é ágoosį? — How is the weather (outside how is it)?
Tł'ó'yé gé gótǫ́ǫ́'é. — The weather is bad.
Deesyoł. — It is starting to blow.
Ńyoł. — It is windy.
Łeesh mił ńyoł. — It is blowing dust (dirt with it it is blowing).
K'os. — It is cloudy.
K'os silį́į́. — It became cloudy.
Dá k'os'é. — It is really cloudy.
Idiłch'ił. — There is lightning.
Idiiníí. — There is thunder.
Dák'aa nkee gółkįįh. — It is about to rain.
Nagoołkįįh. — It is raining.
Nagóółká. — It rained
Iloo naałkįįh. — It is hailing.
Dá iloo'é. — It is icy.
Shóh. — It is frosty.
Dák'aa zas nkee gółkįįh. — It is going to snow soon.
Zas naałkįįh. — It is snowing.
Doo ńdaadé zas naałkįįh. — It is really snowing.
Zas náálká. — It snowed.
Gé godiit'ó. — It is damp, wet weather.
Tł'ó'yé dá gooyéé. — There is fine weather outside.
K'os ésdįį. — The clouds cleared off.
K'os édįį. — It is clear.
Goniidó. — It is going to warm up.
Godndoo. — It warmed up.
Doo ńyoł da. — It is not windy.
Doo goosk'as da. — It is not cold.
Dá goosdo'é. — It is warm.

Use of the *-go* enclitic with weather terms

Ńyołgo doo shił nzhǫ́ da. — I don't like it when it is windy.
Iloo naałkįįhgo doo mił nzhǫ́ da. — He doesn't like it when it hails.
Shóhgo dá gooyéé. — It is beautiful when it is frosty.
Goosdogo shił gózhǫ́. — I am happy when it is warm.

The distributive plural *-da-*, *-daa-*

Da- or *-daa-* is prefixed or infixed to nouns or verbs to denote plurality of more than two. It is varied in its position in verb complexes and often alters form. Its use is to be learned through experience.

Idlą́. — He, she, they (two) drink.
Da'idlą́. — They (more than two) drink.

Miighą. — His, her, their (two) home.
Daamiighą. — Their (more than two) home.

Yéoniisįį. — He, she, they (two) are learning it.
Yédaoniisįį. — They (more than two) are learning it.

Handling verbs

The stem *-lé* refers to the handling of a slender, flexible object, or two such objects:

Tł'ół sha ńlé. — Give me the rope (or string).
Zháał sha ńlé. — Give me the money (two bills only).
Sis sha ńlé. — Give me the belt.

Use the appropriate stem:

Gahée...   Ǫǫzhazhį́į́...
Łeet'áan...   Tł'ół...
Sis...   Kóh...
Káził...   Bésh...
Mósha...

Cultural note

It is not good form among the Jicarilla Apache to ask a person his or her name. Only upon special occasions did the traditional Apache call a person by name. One learned a name through inquiring of a third person. The unauthorized use of a person's name was seen as taking away something personal from that individual. Personal appelations were therefore regarded as property and permission had to be granted by the family for the utterance of one of its names.

One does not call a deceased person by name. It is customary to merely say, *áń édįį'íí* (he or she is gone). And the use of a mother-in-law's name is also taboo. The usual practice of address to an older person is *shii'máá* (my mother) or *shiitsóóyéé* (my grandfather), to a younger person *shiishdázha* (my younger sister or brother), or, in general, *shiich'oonií* (my friend).

A selective comparison of some Apachean terms

It is going to snow soon.

Jicarilla:	Dák'aa zas nkee gółkįįh.
Mescalero:	Ndásu' zas íí naałtįįh.
Western:	Dák'azhą́ zas nkełtįįh.
Navajo:	T'áadoo hodina'í doochííł.

Unit 17 ◀◀◀◀

Dialog

Ha'go kéesda nkee gózhísh? — When will the feast begin?
Kéesda naakiigo nkee gózhísh. — The feast begins at two o'clock.

Ha'dą́ kéesda nkee gózhiizh? — When did the feast begin?
Kái'iidą́ nkee gózhiizh. — It started at three o'clock.

He dák'adéé égóósdįį? — Is it about to end?
Hádą́ égóósdįį. — It already ended.

He kéesda égóósdįį? — Did the feast end?
Díí'iidą́ égóósdįį. — It ended at four o'clock.

Vocabulary

1. ha'go — when (future time)
2. nkee — start, begin
3. gózhísh — time passes
4. naakiigo — at two o'clock (future time)
5. ha'dą́ — when (past time)
6. gózhiizh — time passed
7. kái'iidą́ — at three (past time)
8. dák'adéé — about to, almost, soon
9. égóósdįį — it ends
10. hádą́ — already
11. díí'iidą́ — at four o'clock (past time)

Explanations

1. *Nkee* is an inceptive particle meaning *start, begin*. It is common in Navajo as *niki-(nikee)*.

2. *Naakiigo* (when it is two) implies *two o'clock*, present or future time. If the reference is to two o'clock past time, *naakiidą́*, the past-time marker *-dą́* is appended.

3. Traditionally, the Jicarilla Apache used only the approximations of sunrise, morning, noon or *ha'íí'ągo, nłdągo, iłní'ch'iń'ągo* and so on until night *(tł'é'go)* to refer to the diurnal periods of time.

4. *Gózhísh* and *gózhiizh* are used to express the passage of time. *Nkee gózhísh* might be loosely interpreted as *it starts as time passes* and *nkee gózhiizh* as *it starts as time passed.* This concept is widely employed in all of the Apachean languages. Compare Navajo *k'ad deesdoigo hoolzhish* (literally *now when it is hot, time passes,* i.e., *there is a period of hot weather now*).

5. Contrast *ha'dą́* (when) with *hádą́* (already).

6. *Égóósdįį* conveys a sense of expiration or running out. It is related to *édįį* (non-existent, deceased). It can be compared to Navajo *ásdįįd,* as in *chidí bitoo' sits'ą́ą' ásdįįd* (The gas from me it ran out, i.e., I ran out of gas).

Review and practice with new vocabulary

1. Ha'go godas nkee gózhísh? — When does the pow-wow begin?
   Dákoo nkee gózhiizh. — It is beginning now.

2. He kéesda nkee gózhiizh? — When did the feast begin?
   Doo nkee gózhiizh. — It hasn't begun.

3. He godas dák'adéé égóósdįį? — Is the pow-wow about to end?
   Hádą́ égóósdįį. — It has already ended.

4. Dá'kwíí heńkéés? — What time is it?
   Ashdle' heńkéés. — It is five o'clock.

5. Dá'kwíídą́ kéesda égóósdįį? — What time did the feast end?
   Nóóst'éídą́ heńkéés égóósdįį. — It ended at nine o'clock.

   Note the use of *-dą́* in number 5 above to indicate past time.

6. Dákoo dá'kwíí heńkéés? — What time is it now?
   Naakii iłníích'į heńkéés. — It is two-thirty.

7. Ha'yé n'deeshchíí? — Where were you born?
   Lósii'yé shii'deeshchíí. — I was born in Dulce.

8. N'máá ha'yé mii'deeshchíí? — Where was your mother born?
   Chama'yé mii'deeshchíí. — She was born in Chama.

9. Ha'yéną́ą nénsai? — Where did you grow up?
    Įį'ee néésai. — I grew up here.

10. Nshdázha ha'yé neesai? — Where did your sister grow up?
    Ináaso'yé neesai. — She grew up in Ignacio.

11. Dá'kwíí neeshį́į́dą́ isgwéela'yé nasínyá? — How old were you when you went to school?
    Goskáan sheeshį́į́dą́ isgwéela'ye naséyá. — I was six years old when I went to school.

    Note the use of -dą́ in number 11 above to indicate past age.

12. He godasyé dínyá? — Are you going to the pow-wow?
    Aoo, ha'íí'ą́go déyá. — Yes, I am going at sunrise.

13. Iyáná' ádaał'į́í godas ee? — What do they do at the pow-wow?
    Hadashdii'éí shį́į dashdiidlo. — They sing and they dance.

    Note the use of the distributive plural -da(a)- in the two sentences in number 13 above.

14. He ndékéé ma ńdéí? — Are you going to visit friends?
    Aoo, ma nshéí. — Yes, I am going to visit them (go to them).

15. He nk'éé ma ńdéí? — Are you going to visit relatives?
    Shii'á éí ya híídéí. — My wife is going to visit them.

16. Ha'ń ma ńnyá? — Whom did you visit?
    Shii'máá ma néyá. — I visited my mother.
    Miishdázha ya ńyá. — She visited her sister.

17. Kįį hishdleesh. — I am painting the house.
    He kįį ndleesh? — Are you painting the house?
    Kįį yidleesh. — He is painting the house.

18. He kįį shíńdléésh? — Did you paint the house?
    Aoo, éí shédléésh. — Yes, I painted it.
    Bííł yiishdléésh. — He painted the car.

82

19. Na'ishkǫ́go hásht'íí. — I want to swim.
    He na'iłkǫ́go hánt'íí? — Do you want to swim?
    Na'iłkǫ́go yííkát'íí. — She wants to swim.

20. Na'séłkǫ́. — I swam.
    He na'sínłkǫ́? — Did you swim?
    Na'iiskǫ́. — He swam.

21. Ha'dish'éí. — I am singing.
    He ha'ń'éígo hánt'íí? — Do you want to sing?
    Ha'dii'éígo yííkát'íí. — He wants to sing.

22. Ha'déé'ą́. — I sang.
    Dííshą, ha'dín'ą́? — How about you, did you sing?
    Dooda, ha'dń'ą́. — No, he sang.

23. Ha'ń bííł nailo? — Who is driving the car?
    Shíí bííł naashło. — I am driving the car.
    He bííł naíílo hánt'íí? — Do you want to drive the car?

24. Ha'ń bííł naaslo? — Who drove the car?
    He bííł nasínlo? — Did you drive the car?
    Shíí bííł nasélo. — I drove the car.

Comprehension

Lósii'yé shii'deeshchíí. Á'ee néésai. Shiishdázha gó ą́'ee mii'deeshchíí shíí ą́'ee neesai. Goskáan meeshíídą́ isgwéela'yé naasyá. Yiską́o shiik'éé ma nshéí. Blanco'yé daamiighą.

Questions

1. Ha'yé mii'deeshchíí? — Where was she born?
2. Ha'yé neesai? — Where did she grow up?
3. He miishdázha Lósii'yé mii'deeshchíí? — Was her sister born in Dulce?
4. Ha'dą́ isgwéela'yé naasyá? — When did she go to school?
5. Ha'ń ya híídéí? — Whom is she going to visit?
6. Ha'yé miik'éé daamiighą? — Where are her relatives' homes?

Times of the day

Ha'go nkee gózhísh? — When will it begin?
Ha'íí'ágo — At sunrise
Nłdá'go — In the morning
Iłních'i'ń'ágo — At noon
Iidees'ágo — In the afternoon
Shá'íí'ágo — At sunset
Tł'é'go — At night

Positional verb stems

As with handling verb stems, positional stems define the shape or quality of the object, animate or inanimate, whose position or location is being indicated. The stem -'á refers to a roundish or squarish, bulky, hard object in position. The singular verb form is si'á:

Įį'eeshíí tł'é'na'áí dá aada'é si'á. — The moon is far from here.
Jooł įį'ee chish miiyaayé si'á. — The ball is here under the tree.
Łeet'áan ndééch'į si'á. — The bread is over there.

Animate objects lying in position are referred to with the stem -kíí. The complete 3rd person singular verb form is sikíí:

Mósha ndé'ee sikíí. — The cat is lying over there.
Shii'máá įį'ee sikíí. — My mother is lying here.
Chíníí ndééch'į sikíí. — The dog is over there.

Use the appropriate stem:

Gwii'…   Bóó…
Bésh..,   Kózis…
Itsįį…   Shash…

Both of… and *All of…*

Dá łíńt'an na'iidzii. — Both of us are working.
Dá aniłtso nada'iidzii. — All of us are working.
He *dá'łína'an* dá'kwéé dá'ásh? — Are both of you going there?
He *anałtso* dá'kwéé dákai. — Are all of you going there?

Dá'łéé'an k'e'diilé. — Both of them are planting.
Dá ałtso k'e'da'diilé. — All of them are planting.

Cultural note

Kéesda, the feast, is a time of getting together for food and conversation. Traditional food and drink are prepared in great quanitities. *Káził, ts'íiłiłii,* and *kółbáíí* are consumed jovially, usually in an open country setting, mountain or meadow. *Godas,* the pow-wow, is a gathering of the people for traditional dancing and singing. Both occasions are used to visit with family and friends.

A selective comparison of some Apache terms

Where were you born?

Jicarilla:	Ha'yé n'deeshchíí?
Mescalero:	Ha'yá gusínlįį?
Western:	Hayú gosínlíí?
Navajo:	Háadish ni'dizhchí?

Unit 18   ◄ ◄ ◄ ◄

Dialog

Ha'go nádndééh? — When do you get up?
Goskáango nádiishdééh. — I get up at six.

Dáoshą iiyá'? — Then what?
Ká'ádiisgis. — I wash up.

Dáoshą iiyá'? — Then what?
Bííł iłchíń naiyé'íí mííká sézįį. — I wait for the school bus.

Adáádą ha'dą nádindzá? — When did you get up yesterday?
Ashdle'dą nádiisdzá. — I got up at five.

Ádą́ą́ iyáná' ánlaa? — Then what did you do?
Na'iisii'yé naséyá. — I went to work.

Hat'éonáą dá'kwéé nasínyá? — How did you go there?
Dá nii' naséyá. — I went on foot.

Vocabulary

1. nádndééh — you get up, arise
2. goskáango — at six
3. nádiishdééh — I get up
4. ká'ádiisgis — I wash up
5. dáoshą — and then
6. iiyá' — what
7. bííl iłchíń naiyé'íí — school bus
8. mííká — for it
9. sézįį — I stand
10. adáádą — yesterday
11. nádindzá — you got up
12. ashdle'go — at five
13. ádą́ą́ — then
14. ánlaa — you did
15. na'iisii'yé — to work, to my job
16. hat'éonáą — how, in what manner
17. dá'kwéé — to there
18. dá nii' — on foot, walking

86

Explanations

1. In the terms *nádndééh* and *nádiishdééh* the verbal prefix *ná-* indicates repetition of an action. The verbs may be translated in a literal sense as *you get up again* and *I get up again*. Compare with Navajo *nínádii'nah* and *nínádiish'nah* and Western Apache *nádndáh* and *nádishdáh*.

2. *Bííł iłchíń naiyé'íí* (school bus) is rendered literally as *car children the one that carries them.*

3. *Mííká sézíí* (I wait for it) carries the verbatim meaning *for it I stand*. Also used in everyday vernacular are *mííká sédá* (for it I sit) and *mííká ásht'íí* (for it I am). The postposition *mííká* and verb may be changed to reflect person waiting and person or thing waited for. Thus, *shííká sizíí* (he, she is waiting for me), *nká sézíí* (I am waiting for you), *yííká sizíí* (he, she is waiting for him, her, it). Contrast Navajo *biba' sédá* (I am waiting for him, her) and Western Apache *shiba' síńdaa* (wait for me).

4. The expression *dá nii'* (walking, on foot), means, word-for-word, *just earth*. The Navajos say *t'áá ni'*, with the same meaning.

Review and practice with new vocabulary

1. Nka'éé ha'go nádiidééh? — What time does your father get up?
    Ashdle'go nádiidééh. — He arises at five.

2. Dáoshạ iiyá'? — Then what?
    Ká'ádiigis shíí miishdázha yííká sizíí. — He washes and waits for his brother.

3. N'á ha'dạ́ nádiidzá? — When did your wife get up?
    Goskáango nádiidzá. — She got up at six.

4. Kóńlíí'yé naasyá? — Did she go to the river?
    Kósiłk'ạ'yé naasyá. — She went to the lake.

5. He miibíilii dá'kwéé yee naasyá? — Did she go there in her car?
    Dá nii' naasyá. — She went on foot.

6. Ha'ń mííká sínzíí? — Whom are you waiting for?
    Shiizeedń mííká sézíí. — I am waiting for my cousin.

87

7. Iyáná' ánł'íí? — What are you doing?
   Gé sédá. — I am just hanging around (just sitting).
   Gé ásht'íí. — I am just loafing about (just am).

8. Kįį'yé déyá dá nii'. — I am going to walk to town.
   Shííká sínzįí! — Wait for me!

9. Nchóó ha'yé naaghá? — Where is your grandmother?
   Ndééch'į sida'íí nilįí. — She is the one sitting over there.

10. Ntsóóyéé ha'yé naaghá? — Where is your grandfather?
    Á'ee naaghá'íí nilįí. — He is the one walking about over there.

11. He adádá nándzá? — Did you return yesterday?
    Gosts'idii yiskádá nánsdzá. — I got back seven days ago.

12. Tł'ół sha ńlé. — Give me the rope.
    Aoo, éí na nshłé. — Yes, I'll give it to you.

13. Shiich'į ná'ńlé. — Pay me.
    Aoo, nch'į ná'nshłé. — Yes, I'll pay you.

14. Ha'dá dikosdéé ne'ńłde? — When did you catch cold?
    Adádá dikosdéé she'ńłde. — I caught cold yesterday.
    Dinshnii. — I am sick.
    Iizee łe' hásht'íí. — I want some medicine.

15. Ha'yé nghą? — Where is your home?
    Įį'eeshíí náakosii'yéo shiighą. — My home is north of here.

16. Ha'ń nadaadéé? — Who is playing?
    Lósii shįí Chama nadaadéé. — Dulce and Chama are playing.

17. Ha'ń dagoozo? — Who will win?
    Lósii dagoozo. — Dulce will win.

18. Ha'ń dagóózo? — Who won?
    Lósii dagóózo. — Losii won.

19. He naandéé? — Are you playing (going to play)?
    Doo naashdéé da. — I am not playing.

20. He nshdázha naadéé? — Is your brother going to play?
     Aoo, naadéé. — Yes, he is going to play.

21. He nasíndéé? — Did you play?
     Aoo, nasédéé. — Yes, I played.
     Bíí gó naasdéé. — He played, too.

22. Tł'é'dą dá goosk'as'é n̆t'éé. — It was really cold last night.
     Aoo, dákoo zas dáłánéé. — Yes, now there is a lot of snow.

23. Díijíí k'os édii. — Today there are no clouds.
     Aoo, náoniido. — Yes, it is warming up.

24. Nzhǫgo nandágo. — Take care of yourself (walk about carefully).
     Aoo, díí gó ąą. — Yes, you too.

Comprehension

Jíídą ashdle'dą nádiisdzá. Díijíí godasyé déyá. Á'ee hadashdii'éí áshíí dashdiidlo. Godas goskáango nkee gózhísh. Dáan dáłánéé góníí. Godasyé dá shił hooyéé. Shiidékéé shíí shiik'éé ma nshéí. Shii'á miich'ooníí ya híídéí.

Questions

1. Ha'dą nádiidzá? — When did he get up?
2. Ha'yé deeyá díijíí? — Where is he going today?
3. Godasyé iyáná' ádaał'íí? — What do they do at a pow-wow?
4. Ha'go godas nkee gózhísh? — When does the the pow-wow begin?
5. He dáan góníí? — Is there food?
6. Ha'ń ma híídéí? — Whom is he going to visit?
7. Ha'ń mii'á ya híídéí? — Whom is his wife going to visit?

Imperatives in the negative

Doo yánłkii! — Don't talk!
Doo na'íízii! — Don't work!
Doo ídlą! — Don't drink!
Doo kédandágo! — Don't hurt yourself!

Expressions of emotions

Dá shííná sédá. — I am lonely (I sit alone).
Noosáné. — I like you.
Hoosáné. — I like him, her.
Shoosáné. — He, she likes me.
He shoonsáné? — Do you like me?
Nkásht'íí. — I love you (I want you).
Yííkát'íí. — He loves her, she loves him.
Nee diishnii. — I hate you.
Mee diishnii. — I hate him, her.
Shee diinii. — He, she hates me.
Yee diinii. — He hates him, her.

Handling verbs

The stem -kįį is used to describe the handling of a slender stiff object such as a cigarette, shovel, or cane:

Nát'ohdii sha ńkįį. — Give me the cigarette.
Gish sha ńkįį. — Give me the cane.
Chish sha ńkįį. — Give me the stick.
Łógee mehadloo'íí sha ńkįį. — Give me the fishing pole.

Use the appropriate stem:

Tł'ół…	Gish…
Gahée…	Kóh…
Bésh…	Chíníí…
Mósha…	Nát'ohdii…

Positional verbs

Siká is a verb used to describe something in position in an open container.

Kóh ha'yé siká? — Where is the water?
Miiká'dahch'iyą'íí miiyaayé siká. — It is under the table.
K'edahiisdá'íí miikáá'ee dah siká. — It is on the chair (whereon one sits).
K'edahiisdá'íí miide'shíí siká. — It is behind the chair.

Miiká'dahch'iyá'íí miiláach'įshíį siką́. — It is in front of the table.

Kéłts'ei miigha miiye'yé siką́. — It is in the cupboard (dish house).

Cultural note

The Jicarilla Apache do not have the extensive clan system perpetuated by the Western Apache and the Navajo, these two tribes counting some sixty or more clans each. The Jicarilla tribe is made up of two bands, the Llaneros, or Plains People, and the Olleros, called the Sand People. The Llaneros traditionally lived east of the Rio Grande and the Olleros west of the river. The two bands have always considered themselves one people and are culturally and linguistically identical. In September of each year they proclaim their unity by joining in a relay race and other ceremonials, as well as in traditional feasting, singing, and dancing.

A selective comparison of some Apachean terms

Is there food?

Jicarilla:	He dáan góníí?
Mescalero:	Ha dáne gú'lii?
Western:	Ya' idáń gólį́į?
Navajo:	Da' ch'iyáán hólǫ́?

Unit 19 ◀◀◀◀

Dialog

Ha'yénáá dínyá? — Where are you going?
Biilii há déyá. — I am going after a blanket.

Biilii ha'yé siłtsoos? — Where is the blanket?
Ts'ísk'eh miikáá'yé shíí. — Probably on the bed.

He nádnłtsoos? — Did you get it?
Aoo, nádeełtsoos. — Yes I got it.

Ha'yénáá siłtsoos ńt'éé? — Where was it?
Nii'yé siłtsoos ńt'éé. — It was on the floor.

Vocabulary

1. biilii — blanket
2. há — for it, after it
3. déyá — I am going
4. siłtsoos — it is lying in position
5. ts'ísk'eh — bed
6. miikáá'yé — on it
7. shíí — probably
8. nádnłtsoos — you got it
9. nádeełtsoos — I got it
10. nii'yé — on the floor, ground

Explanations

1. *Há déyá* means *I am going for it, I am going after it.* This phrase may be used to express the concept of going after any undifferentiated object.

2. The verb *nádeełtsoos* is translated as *I got it (a flat, flexible object)* and is therefore, with its stem -(*ł*)*tsoos*, specific to the handling of an object whose qualities are flat and flexible.

3. *Shíí* has four meanings: *and, probably, summer* and, as an enclitic, *from.*

4. The singular future and perfective (past tense) of the verb *to get it (a flat, flexible object)* are as follows. Note the difference in the stems of the two tenses:

Future
nádiistsós — I shall get it
nádinłtsós — you will get it
náidiiłtsós — he, she will get it

Perfective
nádeełtsoos — I got it
nádinłtsoos — you got it
náidiiłtsoos — he, she got it

Review and practice with new vocabulary

1. Ha'yé dínyá? — Where are you going?
   Ísee há déyá — I am going for the bowl.

2. He ísee nádn'ą? — Did you get the bowl?
   Aoo, nádee'ą. — Yes, I got it.

3. He nshdázha bésh náidin'ą? — Did your sister get the knife?
   Dooda, shíí nádee'ą. — No, I got it.

4. He n'á gahée náidinką. — Did your wife get the coffee?
   Dooda, shíí nádeeką. — No, I got it.

5. He kóh nádnką? — Did you get the water?
   Dooda, shii'á náidinką. — No, my wife got it.

6. He naałtsoozii nádnłtsoos? — Did you get the sheet of paper?
   Shiichóó náidiiłtsoos. — My grandmother got it.

7. He ik'e'íílchíí? — Are you writing?
   Aoo, ik'e'ishchíí. — Yes, I am writing.
   Bíí gó ik'e'iłchíí. — She is writing, too.

8. He ik'e'shínłchíí? — Did you write?
   Aoo, ik'e'shéłchíí. — Yes, I wrote.
   Bíí gó ik'e'iishchíí. — She also wrote.

9. He ónłkai? — Are you reading?
   Aoo, óshkai. — Yes, I am reading.
   Bíí gó ółkai. — He is reading, too.

10. Adą́ą́dą́ óołkai. — I read yesterday.
    Dííshą, he óonłkai? — How about you, did you read?
    Shiiną'ą́ą́ óołkai. — My older brother read.

11. He bił ńńzįį? — Are you sleepy?
    Aoo, bił nsįį. — Yes, I am sleepy.
    Bíí gó bił ńzįį. — He too is sleepy.

12. He iłhoshgo hánt'íí? — Do you want to sleep?
    Ishhoshgo hásht'íí. — I want to sleep.
    Bíí gó iłhoshgo yííkát'íí. — She wants to sleep, too.

13. He iinłhaash? — Did you sleep?
    Doo eełhaash da. — I didn't sleep.
    Shiika'éé iiłhaash. — My father slept.

14. Diishdlo hásht'íí. — I want to dance.
    He díídlogo hánt'íí? — Do you want to dance?
    Dooda, diidlogo yííkát'íí. — No, he wants to dance.

15. Déédlo. — I danced.
    Dííshą, dińdlo? — How about you, did you dance?
    Dooda, shiizhách'į'íí diidlo. — No, my daughter danced.

16. He íídéńká? — Are you going to run?
    Aoo, íídéenshká. — Yes, I am going to run
    Bíí gó íídéenká. — She is going to run, too.

17. Íídénééką́. — I ran.
    Dííshą, he íídéńínką́? — How about you, did you run?
    Dooda, shiiną'ą́ą́ íídeneeská. — No, my older brother ran.

18. He hiiskasgo hánt'íí? — Do you want to run?
    Aoo, hiskasgo hásht'íí. — Yes, I want to run.
    Bíí gó hikasgo yííkát'íí . — She also wants to run.

19. He nasínkaas? — Did you run?

94

Doo nasékaas da. — I didn't run.

Shiiyii'íí naskaas. — My son ran.

20. Iyáná' hííyínłts'á? — What are you listening to?

    Abáachii ha'dii'éí hííyésts'á. — I am listening to Apache songs.

    Bíí gó yííyests'á. — She also is listening to them.

21. Iyáná' híísínłts'á? — What did you listen to?

    Yáłkii'íí hííyééłts'á. — I listened to a speech.

    Abáachii miiyin hííyeests'á. — He listened to Apache songs.

22. N'á ha'go nádiidééh? — What time does your wife arise?

    Tseebíígo nádiidééh. — She gets up at eight.

23. He miich'ooníí yííká sizíí? — Does she wait for her friend?

    Aoo, ła'go yííká sizíí. — Yes, she sometimes waits for her.

24. Nzeedń ha'dá nádiidzá? — When did your cousin get up?

    Díí'iidá nádiidzá. — She got up at four.

25. Ha'yé haskįįyíí Vigil miighą? — Where is Mr. Vigil's home?

    Dá adaahégo si'á. — It is farther on.

    Áháánégo si'á. — It is closer in.

26. Ha'shíí naaghá? — Where does he come from?

    Dá aadahéshíí naaghá. — He comes from farther on.

    Dá áháánéshíí naaghá. — He comes from closer in.

27. Iyáná' ánł'íí? — What are you doing?

    Dá shíí shiighą ágoshłé. — I am going build (make) my own house.

    He ntsaago ágólé? — Are you going to build a large one?

    Aoo, tsé mee ágoshłé. — Yes, I'll make it out of stone.

    Shiika'éé kįį chish mee ágolé. — My father is building one of wood.

28. Iyáná' ánlaa? — What did you do?

    Kįį ágoshłaa. — I built a house.

    Dííshą, he kįį ágonlaa? — How about you, did you build a house?

    Shiiną'áá kįį ágolaa. — My older brother built a house.

29. He nka'éé má na'íízii ńt'éé? — Were you working for your father?

    Aoo, énda dákoo égóósdįį. — Yes, but now it is finished.

30. Éí miighą iyáná' mee áyaa? — What is his house made of?
    Chish mee áyaa. — It is made of wood.

Comprehension

Dzilyé déyá. Tł'ó'yé dá goosk'as'é. Zas dáłánéé nii'yé góníí. Chish há déyá. Áshį́į́
de'diishjee shiighą'yé. Áshį́į́ naałtsoozii hóshkai hásht'į́į́. Shii'á ik'e'iłchíí yííkát'íí.

Questions

1. Ha'yé deeyá? — Where is he going?
2. Tł'ó'yé hat'éo ágoosį? — How is the weather?
3. He zas nii'yé góníí? — Is there snow on the ground?
4. Iyáná' há deeyá? — What is he going after?
5. He de'diiłjee? — Is he going to build a fire?
6. Ha'yé de'diiłjee? — Where is he going to build a fire?
7. Iyáná' yółkaigo yííkát'íí? — What does he want to read?
8. Mii'á iyáná' áyiił'į́į́go yííkát'íí? — What does his wife want to do?

Positional verbs

As you have observed in this unit, the stems -łtsós and -łtsoos are used to express the
handling of flat, flexible objects such as paper, blankets, and even flat tires. The corre-
sponding positional stem, which is also -łtsoos, is employed to characterize those kinds
of objects lying in position. Remember that *naałtsoozii* means *paper* as well as *book:*

Naałtsoozii kwéé siłtsoos. — The paper is (lying) here.
Naałtsoozii kwéé si'á. — The book is here.
Biilii kwéé siłtsoos. — The blanket is here.
Bíłł miikee kwéé siłtsoos.— The flat tire is here.

Use the appropriate positional stem:

Łį́į́…	Naałtsoozii (sheet of paper)…
Naałtsoozii (book)…	Shii'máá…
Kóh…	Biilii…
Łeet'áan…	Itsįį…

Expressions

Shił godéenííh. — I am angry.

He nł godéenííh? — Are you angry?

Mił godéenííh. — He, she is angry.

Ma ííníínaskees. — I am thinking about it.

He ma ííníínsínłkees? — Are you thinking about it?

Ya ííníínaiłkees. — He, she is thinking about it.

Mą shíínii — I am worried about it (it is alongside my mind).

He mą ńnii? — Are you worried about it?

Yą míínii. — He, she is worried about it.

Doo mą ńnii. — Don't worry about it.

Ma yá nsįį. — I am ashamed of it. I am bashful.

He ma yá ńńzįį? — Are you ashamed of it? Are you bashful?

Ya yá ńzįį. — He, she is ashamed of it. He, she is bashful.

Doo yá ńńzįįgo. — Don't be ashamed. Don't be bashful.

A selective comparison of some Apachean terms

It is good. It is bad.

Jicarilla — Nzhǫ́. Ntǫ́ǫ́'é

Mescalero — Nzhu. Ntu'

Western — Nzhǫǫ. Nchǫ'

Navajo — Nizhóní. Nchǫ́ǫ́'í

Unit 20 ◀◀◀◀

Dialog

He haskįįyíí Vigil miiyii'íí méońsį? — Do you know Mr. Vigil's son?
Aoo, mégosį. — Yes, I know him.
Iyáná'ííká shéna'íídńłkiih? — Why do you ask?

Dałk'iidą́ doo hish'íí da. — I haven't seen him in a long time.
He míízhii ménánłnii? — Do you remember his name?

Doo ménáshnii da. — I don't remember it.
Ménásisdee. — I forgot it (have forgotten it).
Dałk'iidą́ kwéé miighą́ ńt'éé. — He lived here a long time ago.

Įį'ee dá'kwíí hai nee goslį́į? — How long have you lived here?
Naadin hai kwéé shee goslį́į. — I have lived here for twenty years.

Vocabulary

1. haskįįyíí — man, Mr.
2. miiyii'íí — his son
3. méońsį — you know him
4. mégosį — I know him
5. iyáná'ííká — why
6. shéna'íídńłkiih — you ask me
7. dałk'iidą́ — for a long time, a long time ago
8. doo hish'íí da — I don't see him
9. míízhii — his name
10. ménánłnii — you remember it
11. ménáshnii — I remember it
12. ménásisdee — I forgot it
13. kwéé — here, hereabouts
14. miighą — his home
15. ńt'éé — a marker of past time
16. įį'ee — here
17. dá'kwíí — how many, how much
18. hai — winter(s), year(s)
19. nee goslį́į — you have lived
20. naadin — twenty
21. shee goslį́į — I have lived

Explanations

1. *Haskįįyįį* means *man*. When used with a surname it implies English *Mr.* *Shiihaskįįyįį* is translated as *my husband*. This term may be likened to Mescalero *shighaastį* and Navajo *shihastiin*.

2. The first three persons of the verb *to know him, her, it* are *mégosį, méońsi, yégósį*. The prefixed direct object pronouns of this verb may be manipulated to change meaning: *négosį* (I know you), *shégósį* (he knows me), *négósį* (she knows you). Compare these forms with Navajo *bééhasin, bééhonísin, yééhósin*. Moreover, contrast Jicarilla Apache *to know him, it, her* with the forms for *to become acquainted with him, her, it*, or, as you have seen in previous units, *to learn it:*

   mégosį — I know him   méoniisįį — I am learning it
   méońsį — you know him   méońsįį — you are learning it
   yégósį — he knows him   yéoniisįį — he is learning it

2. *Dałk'iidą́ doo hish'įį da* (I haven't seen him in a long time) may be rendered literally as *long time (ago) I do not see him*.

3. *Dałk'iidą́ kwéé miighą ńt'éé* (he lived here a long time ago) has the verbatim meaning *long ago ḣere his home was*.

4. The question *įį'ee dá'kwíí hai nee goslįį?* (How long have you lived here?) is highly idiomatic, meaning literally *here how many winters with you it came into existence*. The verb *goslįį* (it became, came into existence) may be compared with Navajo *hazlį́į'*, as in *awéé' hazlį́į'* (a baby was born), or *k'os (da)hazlį́į'* (it became cloudy).

5. A literal interpretation of the phrase *naadin hai kwéé shee goslįį* is *twenty winters here with me it became*. Navajo *naadiin ńááhai* is related with its use of *hai* as *year*, but translates as *twenty repeated winters*.

Review and practice with new vocabulary

1. He iisdzą́níí Chavez méońsį? — Do you know Mrs. (Woman) Chavez?
   Doo mégosį da. — I don't know her.
   Shii'á yégósį. — My wife knows her.

2. Ha'yé miighą? — Where is her home?
   Dałk'iidą́ įį'ee miighą. — She lived here a long time ago.

99

3. Miihaskįyį́į́ hat'éo mį́ízhii ? — What was her husband's name?
   Doo ménáshnii da. — I don't remember.

4. He ménásínłdee? — Did you forget it.
   Aoo, ménásisdee. — Yes, I forgot it.

5. Iyáná' mee gonii? — What is going on (what's new?)?
   Koghą ágoshłé. — I am building a house.

   Note: Compare low-toned *gonii* (news, story) in number 5 above with high-toned *góníí* (it exists). A literal rendering of *iyáná' mee gonii?* is *what with it the news?*, free translation, *what is going on, what's new?*

6. He ánł'į́į́ dá meońsį? — Do you know how to do it?
   Aoo, ásh'į́į́ dá mégosį. — Yes, I know how to do it.

7. Iyáná' mee gonii? — What is going on?
   Abáachii méoniisįį. — I am learning Apache.

8. He Abáachii dáłánéé nł mégózįį? — Do you know much about Apache?
   Aoo, Abáachii dá shił mégózįį. — Yes, I know about it.

9. Nka'éé įį'ee dá'kwíí hai mee goslį́í? — How long has your father lived here?
   Gonesnáan hai įį'ee mee goslį́í. — He has lived here for ten years.

10. Iyáná' nínł'į́í? — What are you looking at?
    Ndé'ee łį́í sizį́í'íí nésh'į́í. — I'm looking at that horse standing over there.

11. Iyáná' yinééł'į́í? — What is he looking at?
    Ndé'ee iisdzáníí sidá'íí yinééł'į́í. — He's looking at that woman sitting over there.

12. He gé ánt'į́í? — Are you just loafing around?
    Aoo, gé ásht'į́í. — Yes, I am just loafing about.
    Gé át'į́í bíí gó. — She is just loafing around also.

13. He dééh nłbésh? — Are you boiling tea?
    Káził hishbésh. — I am boiling stew.
    Gahée yiłbésh. — She is boiling coffee.

14. Dééh shéłbésh. — I boiled tea.
    He gahée shínłbésh? — Did you boil coffee?
    Dooda, bíí gahée yiishbésh. — No, he boiled coffee.

100

15. Dá likạ'égo gołchị — It smells good.
    Aoo, dá likạ'é. — Yes, it's tasty.

16. Iyáná' nłt'ees? — What are you frying?
    Itsịị hist'ees. — I am frying meat.
    Łógee yiłt'ees. — He is frying fish.

17. Bába séłt'é. — I fried potatoes.
    He łógee sínłt'é? — Did you fry fish?
    Dooda, bíí łógee yiist'e. — No, she fried fish.

18. He łịį naaniiyégo hánt'íí? — Do you want to ride a horse?
    Aoo, łịį naashiiyégo hásht'íí. — I want to ride a horse.
    Łịį namiiyégo yííkát'íí bíí gó. — She too wants to ride a horse.

19. Adạ́dạ́ naasiisyíí. — I rode yesterday.
    He adạ́dạ́ naaniisyíí? — Did you ride yesterday?
    Adạ́dạ́ shiiyii'íí naamiisyíí. — My son rode yesterday.

20. Łịį ha'yé sizíígo át'é ńńzịị? — Where do you think the horse is?
    Shiikéyaa'yé sizíígo át'é nsịị. — I think it's on my land.
    Miikéyaa'yé sizíígo át'é ńzịị. — He thinks it's on his land.

21. Ík'ạ́ạ́'yé naashágo dá shił hooyéé. — I like to walk (wander) in the hills.
    He ík'ạ́ạ́'yé nandágo dá nł hooyéé? — Do you like to wander in the hills?
    Shii'á ík'ạ́ạ́'yé naaghágo dá mił hooyéé. — My wife likes to walk in the hills.

22. Iyáná' ntł'ół? — What are you weaving?
    Biilii hishtł'ół. — I am weaving a blanket
    Biilii yitł'ół bíí gó. — She too is weaving a blanket.

23. He biilii síntł'ół? — Did you weave the blanket?
    Dooda, éí doo sétł'ół da. — No, I didn't weave it.
    Shiidádéé éí yiistł'ół. — My older sister wove it.

Comprehension

Haskịịyíí Vicenti mégosị, énda dałk'iidạ́ doo hish'íí da. Dákoo Ináaso'yé miighạ. Áń
ịị'ee dałk'iidạ́ miighạ ńt'éé. Naadin hai kwéé mee goslíí.

101

Questions

1. Ha'ń yégósį? — Whom does he know?
2. He dałk'iidą́ doo yaa'íí da? — Hasn't he seen him recently?
3. Dákoo ha'yé miigha? — Where does he live now?
4. Dá'kwíí hai kwéé mee goslį́į́? — How long did he live here?

More handling verbs

The stem used in the imperfective in reference to a flat, flexible object is *-łtsós:*
Biilii sha ńłtsós. — Give me the blanket.

The stem for imperfective handling verbs involving plural, separable objects is *-jéí.*
Mansáana sha ńjéí. — Give me the apples.

Use the appropriate stem:

Bésh...   Nát'ohdii...

Mósha...   Naałtsoozii (sheet of paper)...

Mósha (plural)...   Chíníí...

Kóh...

More positional verbs

The positional verb used in reference to a slender, stiff object is *siką́,* the same verb that is used for liquid in an open container:

Įį'ee gish siką́. — The cane is here.
Įį'ee kóh siką́. — The water is here.

The positional verb employed in reference to a slender, flexible object is *sila:*

Ha'yé sis silá? — Where is the belt?

Use the appropriate positional stem:

Chish...   Łį́į́...

Bésh...   Káził...

Tł'ół...   Biilii...

Expressions

Nááná shíí da. — It is my turn.
Nááná díí da. — It is your turn.
Nááná bíí da. — It is his, her turn.
Dákoo shíí da nááná. — It is my turn now.
He kédíndá? — Did you hurt yourself?
Kédéédá. — I hurt myself.
Kédńdá. — He hurt himself.
Dák'adéé daatsei. — He is going to die.
Daatsei. — He is dying.
Daastsá. — He died.

A selective comparison of some Apachean terms

It happened a long time ago.

Jicarilla: Dałk'iidą́ ágodzaa.
Mescalero: Dáałk'idą́ águudzaa.
Western: Iłk'ihíná' ágodzaa.
Navajo: Ałk'idą́ą́' áhoodzaa.

Unit 21　◀◀◀◀

Dialog

Ha'go ńdéí? — When will you arrive?
Naakii yiskágo nshéí. — I'll arrive in two days.

N'máá ha'goną́ą híídéí? — When will your mother arrive?
Yiskágo iidees'ágo híídéí. — She will come tomorrow afternoon.

Ha'dą́ ńnyá? — When did you arrive?
Adą́dą́ néyá. — I arrived yesterday.

Nchóó ha'dą́ ńyá? — When did your grandmother arrive?
Dį́į́'ii yiską́dą́ ńyá. — She came four days ago.

Vocabulary

1. ńdéí — you will arrive
2. nshéí — I shall arrive
3. híídéí — he, she will arrive
4. naakii yiskágo — in two days
5. iidees'ágo — in the afternoon

6. ńnyá — you arrived
7. néyá — I arrived
8. ńyá — he, she arrived
9. dį́į́'ii yiską́dą́ — four days ago

Explanations

1. *Yiską́* means *the night has passed, it has dawned.* With the enclitic *-go (yiskágo),* the literal connotation is *when the night has passed. Naakii yiskágo,* therefore, is rendered as *when two nights have passed,* i.e., *in two days.*

2. *Dį́į́'ii yiską́dą́* (four days ago) carries the verbatim meaning *four nights passed,* the enclitic *-dą́* being a marker of past time.

3. *Iidees'ágo* (in the afternoon, when it is afternoon) implies early to mid-afternoon. *Iidees'á,* containing the element *-de(i)-* (over, beyond) and the stem *-á* (perfective

of -*ai*), referring to a roundish object having been moved, carried or handled (see Unit 9, Explanations 3, 4, and 5), suggest that the sun has moved beyond the meridian. Compare Mescalero Apache *ya'deeyá* (early afternoon), Western Apache *ha'iz'ąą* (noon), and Navajo *yaa'adeiz'á* (afternoon).

Review and practice with new vocabulary

1. He nzeedń yiskągo híídéí? — Is your cousin arriving tomorrow?
   Doo híídéí da. — He is not coming.

2. He nzhách'į'íí adądą́ ńyá? — Did your daughter arrive yesterday?
   Doo ńyá da. — She did not come.

3. He éí diidé dá méońsį? — Do you know that man?
   Aoo, éí ménáshnii. — Yes, I remember him.

4. Iyáná' nínł'íí? — What are you looking at?
   Doo yá' nésh'íí da. — I'm not looking at anything.

5. Iyáná' ánł'íí? — What are you doing?
   Doo yá' ásh'íí da. — I am not doing anything.
   Gé ásht'íí. — I am just loafing around.

6. Ha'yé dínyá? — Where are you going?
   Doo ha'yé déyá da. — I'm not going anywhere.

7. He é kanángis? — Are you washing clothes?
   Aoo, é kanásgis. — Yes, I am washing clothes.
   Bíí gó é kanáigis. — She too is washing clothes.

8. Kéłts'ei kanáségis. — I washed the dishes.
   Dííshą, he bííł kanásíngis? — Did you wash the car?
   Dooda, shiika'éé bííł kanáyiisgis. — No, my father washed the car.

   Note that the verb in numbers 7 and 8 above may be used to express the washing of any object.

9. Nágogo. — He is going to hoe.
   Shíí gó nágoshgo. — I am going to hoe, too.
   He nángogo? — Are you going to hoe?

10. He naosíngo. — Did you hoe?
    Aoo, naoségo. — Yes, I hoed.
    Bíí gó nágoosgo. — He also hoed.

11. He tł'ó'yé dínyá? — Are you going outside?
    Aoo, tł'ó'yé déyá. — Yes, I am going outside.
    Tł'ó'yé naséyá. — I went outside.
    Tł'ó'yé naasyá. . — He went outside.

Note above that the present tense verb *déyá, dínyá, deeyá* and the past tense verb *naséyá, nasínyá, naasyá* are used to express the idea, present and past, of leaving an enclosure. The examples below illustrate that a different verb is used to indicate entering a building. *Ye'* means *inside* or *into.*

12. Ye' nádééh.— He is going inside.
    Shíí gó ye' náshdééh. — I too am going inside.
    He ye' nándééh? — Are you going inside?

13. He ye' náandzá? — Did you go inside?
    Doo ye' náasdzá da. — I didn't go inside.
    Bíí ye' náadzá. — She went inside.

14. He nchóó miich'oondé? — Are you helping your grandmother?
    Aoo, miich'ooshdé. — Yes, I am helping her.
    Shiishdázha gó yiich'oodé. — My sister is also helping her.

15. Dibé má naniisoo. — I am herding sheep for her.
    Díísha, he dibé nańyoo? — And you, are you herding sheep?
    Shiizeedń dibé nainiiyoo. — My cousin is herding sheep.

16. Adádá dibé nanéyoo. — I herded sheep yesterday.
    He dibé nanínyoo? — Did you herd sheep?
    Shiiyii'íí dibé nainesyoo. — My son herded sheep.

17. He nadá' k'edínlé? — Are you planting corn?
    Bába k'ediishłé. — I am planting potatoes.
    Naayizéé k'eidiilé. — He is planting squash.

18. He naayizéé k'edínlá? — Did you plant squash?
    Nadá' k'edéélá. — I planted corn.
    Bába k'eidńlá. — He planted potatoes.

106

19. Ma ináshdlo. — I am laughing about it.
    He ma inándlo? — Are you laughing about it?
    Ya inádlo. — He is laughing about it.
    Ma'goołkąą. — It is funny.

20. Iishdlo. — I laughed.
    He íindlo? — Did you laugh?
    Bíí iidlo. — He laughed.

21. Ła'go hishcha. — I cry sometimes.
    He ncha? — Are you crying?
    Hiicha. — She is crying.

22. Hécha. — I cried.
    He hiińcha? — Did you cry?
    Óǫzhazhíí hiicha. — The baby cried.

23. He doo nł gózhǫ? — Aren't you happy?
    Doo shił gózhǫ da. — I am not happy.
    Mił gózhǫ. — She is happy.
    Shił gózhǫ ńt'éé. — I used to be happy.

24. Iyáná' nzhǫgo ánlé? — What are you fixing?
    Bííł nzhǫgo áshłé. — I am fixing the car.
    Bíí gó miibíilii nzhǫgo áyiilé. — He is fixing his car, too.

25. He bííł nzhǫgo ánlaa? — Did you fix the car?
    Dooda, doo nzhǫgo áshlaa da. — No, I didn't fix it.
    Bíí éí nzhǫgo áyiilaa. — He fixed it.

26. He nzhǫgo hádikaaz dákoo? — Does it run well now?
    Dooda, shaa k'éts'íłkǫ. — No, it broke down on me.

Comprehension

Díijíí shiich'ooníí híídéí. Kéesda'yé diit'ash. Adądą shii'máá miich'į naséyá. Tł'é'go miighąch'į néyá. Á'ee shee yiiská.

107

Questions

1. Ha'ń híídéí? — Who will arrive?
2. Ha'go híídéí? — When will she arrive?
3. Ha'yé deesh'ash? — Where are the two of them going?
4. Ha'ń miich'į naasyá? — Whom did she go to see?
5. Ha'dą́ ą́ch'į ńyá? — When did she arrive there?
6. Ha'yé mee yiiską́? — Where did she spend the night?

Using the 1st person dual and distributive plural to express *Let's*...

To one other person (1st person dual)

Jooł naadéé. — Let's play ball.
Diidlo. — Let's dance.
Óołkai. — Let's read.
Ik'e'iilchíí. — Let's write.
Dá'kwéé diit'ash. — Let's go there.
Nłį́į' níiłt'į́į. — Let's look at your horse.

To two or more people (distributive plural)

Jooł nadaadéé. — Let's play ball.
Dadiidlo. — Let's dance.
Da'óołkai. — Let's read.
Ik'e'da'iilchíí. — Let's write.
Dá'kwéé diikai. — Let's go there.
Nłį́į' daníiłt'į́į. — Let's look at your horse.

Observe that for the most part in the examples above the distributive plural is based upon the dual forms, the element -*da(a)*- being either prefixed to or infixed within the dual verb. The verb paradigms provided at the end of this book will display the forms necessary for you to construct *Let's*... phrases. With experience and practice you will develop a sense of where -*da(a)*- is placed on or within the dual form if you wish to address more than one other person. Notice that the above *going* verb alters stem rather than using -*da(a)*-. This is not always the case, as you will see in the verb paradigms.

Positional verbs

siłką́ — Used to refer to liquid in position outside a container:
Kóh nii'yé siłką́. — The water is (in a puddle) on the floor.

shijei — For loose, separable objects, or for hay, wool, and so forth:
Naa'oléé ndé'ee shijei. — The beans are over there.
Tł'oh įį'ee shijei. — The hay is here.

sitłé — For mushy matter:
Goshtł'ish ą́'ee sitłé. — The cement (mud) is over there.

si'įį — For several or many objects of varied or unspecified qualities:
Dá'yá'déé ą́'ee si'įį. — Everything is there.

Particles

Chama'yé *dáła'éédii* naséyá. — I went to Chama *once*.
Dáłánéédii heełtsą́. — I saw it *a lot of times*.
Dibé *dáłánéé* ą́'ee góníí n̄t'éé. — There were *many* sheep there.
Kóh siłką́ *dá ałtso'yé.* — There is water *everywhere*.
Dá'łáaná náhiistsé. — I see her *a lot*.
Dá'ałts'íísdégo hásht'įį. — I want *part (a little)* of it.
Łat'įįyéego dá'kwéé déyá. — I'll go *in a little while*.
Dá nááná ha'go na'iisii. — I work *once in a while*.
Įį'ee *dałk'iidą́* na'iisii — I have worked here *for a long time*.
Dá'yá'déé įį'ee si'įį. — *Everything* is here.
Dibé *dá ha'yé* naakai. — Sheep are *everywhere*.
Dibé *dá'iijootyé* naakai. — Sheep are *everywhere*.
Ndééch'į *łe'* dibé góníí. — Over there are *other* sheep.

Personal characteristics

Dá ndeezé. — He is tall.
Gé ałts'íísdé. — He is short.
Dá łik'aa'é. — He is corpulent.
Gé dik'ą́áné. — She is slender.
Dá hooyéé. — He is nice.
Dá hashké'é. — He is mean.

Dá naałwo'é. — He is strong.

Doo naałwo da. — He is weak.

Éí iisdzáníí nzhǫ́. — That woman is beautiful.

Éí haskįįyíí gé ntǫ́ǫ́'é. — That man is homely.

Díí ishkiiyíí ma gózhǫ́. — This boy is good natured

A selective comparison of some Apachean terms

Her mother is young.

Jicarilla: Mii'máá ánii naaghá (she walks about recently).
Mescalero: Bimá ánde' naa'ghá.
Western: Bimá ánii naghaa.
Navajo: Bimá ániid naaghá.

Appendix 1 ◀◀◀◀

Additional Useful Phrases and Questions

1. Ma gózhǫ́. — He, she is good natured.
2. Miijéé dá ntsaayé. — He is kind, big-hearted.
3. Góyą́. — He is intelligent.
4. Íłtsé sidá. — He is patient.
5. Miizháalii dáłánéé. — He is rich.
6. Ke' íísííné. — He is poor.
7. Ke' nsííné. — I am poor.
8. Doo diits'e. — He is mischievous.
9. Má'iits'íí'dé. — He is lucky.
10. Shá'iits'íí'dé. — I am lucky.
11. Icha nchį. — He is stingy.
12. Doo ńdaadé yáłkii. — He talks a lot, too much.
13. Dá naach'áá'é. — He is dishonest. He is a liar.
14. Dá iinii'įį'é. — He is a thief.
15. Miinii naakii. — He is two-faced.
16. Doo ch'oodlą́ da. — Don't believe him.
17. Doo hooshdlą́ da. — I don't believe him, her, it.
18. Néłdzii'íí nilį́í. — He is fearful, cowardly.
19. Dá haííná hashké. — He is quick-tempered.
20. Dá haííná haacha. — He is a crybaby.
21. Éí dá ńkáyé ágoł'į́í. — He acts haphazardly, is foolish.
22. Iida ódlíí. — He is arrogant, proud, a show-off.
23. Gé ntǫ́ǫ́'é. — He is wicked, evil.
24. Miidékéé édįį. — He has no friends.
25. Miik'éé édįį. — He has no relatives (a very negative Apachean saying).

26. Kwé'daką́. — It is open.
27. Doo kwé'daką́ da. — It is closed.
28. Hííłtsei. — It is dry.
29. Ditłé. — It is wet.
30. Tł'ó'yé dá gółtseiyé. — The weather is dry (it is dry outside).
31. Tł'ó'yé dá goditłé'é. — The weather is wet (it is wet outside).
32. Miiye' dáłánéé. — It is full.
33. Miiye' édįį. — It is empty.

34. Dá iilanéé. — It is a busy place.
35. Doo dáo át'é. — It is not so.
36. Ikéé' iislį́į́. — It is late.
37. Shíí iilaa néyá. — I arrived early.
38. Dá aaníí. — It is certain. It is right.
39. Dá éí yeełt'éo. — It is correct.
40. Dá aaníí ádiishníí. — I am right.
41. Doo ásį. — It does not matter.
42. Dá ntsaayé. — It is big.
43. Áłts'íísdé. — It is small.
44. Ánii. — It is new.
45. Háákii. — It is old.
46. Dáłánéé íílį́į́. — It is expensive.
47. Doo łáo íílį́į́ da. — It is inexpensive.
48. Áháánéé. — It is near.
49. Dá aada'é. — It is far.
50. Doo łą́ da. — It is not much. It is a little bit.
51. Dáłánéé. — It is a lot.
52. Dákoo. — It is enough.
53. Dá ą́'ee. — It is enough.
54. Łe'gó nááná. — It is not enough, some more.
55. Dííyéé. — It is yours.
56. Shííyéé. — It is mine.
57. Bííyéé. — It is his, hers.
58. Nahííyéé. — It is ours.
59. He nahííyéé? — Is it yours? (plural)
60. He díí dííyéé át'é? — Is this yours?
61. Díí shííyéé át'é. — This is for me.
62. Díí bííyéé át'é. — This is for him, her.
63. Dá kwéego át'é. — That's the way it is.

64. Dá įį'ee sédá. — I'm staying here.
65. Dákoo déyá. — I have to leave now.
66. He k'adii? — Are you ready?
67. Aoo, k'adii. — Yes, I'm ready.
68. Haííńt'įo. — Hurry up.
69. Dá haííná. — Quickly.
70. Íłtsé. — Wait. Patience.
71. Shił deesh'ash yííkát'į́į. — He wants to go with me.
72. Dá bíína deeyá. — He is going alone
73. Dá shííná déyá. — I am going alone.
74. Dá áshłé. — It is necessary that I do it.

75. Dá shííná déyágo dá áshłé. — I have to go alone.
76. Abáachii méoniisįįgo dá áshłé. — It is necessary that I learn Apache.

77. Doo dákoo ánlaa da. — You made a mistake.
78. Doo dákoo áshłaa da. — I made a mistake.
79. Naałtsoozii shiich'į ánlé. — Show me the book.
80. Nch'į áshłé. — I'll show it to you.
81. Shiich'į áyiilaa. — He showed it to me.
82. Dá sałdii. — They are different.
83. Abáachii shįį Dawoséeo doo iłeełt'é da. — Apache and Taos are not the same.

84. Ha'ńną́ át'į́į? —Who is he, she?
85. Ha'ńną́ ádaat'į́į? — Who are they?
86. Ha'ńną́ áníí? — Who said it?
87. Ha'ńną́ áyiilé? — Who is doing it?
88. Ha'ńną́ áyiilaa? — Who did it?
89. Ha'ńną́ miibíilii át'é? — Whose car is it?
90. Díísha, ha'ńną́ má? — Whom is this for?
91. Ha'ńną́ hiinłtsé hánt'į́í? — Whom do you want to see?
92. Ha'ńną́ yégósį? — Who knows it?
93. Díísha, ha'ńną́ bííyéé? — Whose is this?

94. Iyáná' át'é? — What is it?
95. Díínąą iyáná' át'é? — What is this?
96. Hat'énąą ásį? — What is the matter?
97. Hat'énąą áńńsį? — What is the matter with you?
98. Iyáná' mee gonii? — What's up, what's new?
99. Hat'énąą ádzaa? — What happened?
100. Iyáná' daach'inii? — What's new, what are they saying?
101. Iyáná' nan'įį? — What do you have?
102. Hat'énąą nł ásį? — What do you think, what is your opinion?
103. Iyáná' ádńíí? — What are you saying?
104. Iyáná' díńńíí? — What did you say?
105. Iyáná' ma yánłkii? — What are you talking about?
106. Ma yáshkii. — I'm talking about him, her.
107. Iyáná' ya yáłkii? — What is he talking about?
108. Na yáłkii. — He is talking about you.
109. Iyáná' ma át'é? — What is it all about?

Humor

▼ ▼ ▼ ▼

The following story puns on the low-toned, unglottalized word *miikee* (his, her feet) and high-toned, glottalized *miik'éé* (his, her family or relatives). The Apachean languages are rich in the potential for such word play.

Haskịịyịịzháá	miikee	nchaago	shịị	k'e' diiniigo
little old man	his feet	swollen	and	hurting

háasbila'yé	naasyá.	Áshịị	háasbila'ee	iizee	áyiił'ịị'íí
hospital to	he went	And	hospital at	medicine	she makes it one who

áyiiłníí,	"Ha'nậậ	k'e' diinii,	shiitsóóyéé?"	Áshịị	haskịịyịịzháá
she says	how	it hurts	my grandfather	then	little old man

áyiiłníí,	"Shiikee	nchaa	shịị	k'e' diinii,"	ágołníí.	Iizee
he says	my feet	they swell	and	they hurt	he says	medicine

áyiił'ịị'íí	ánááyiiłníí,	"Haéé'ạ,	shiitsóóyéé,
she makes it one who	she says again	all right	my grandfather

shịị	éí	dákoo	yidóoł	miich'ị	yáshkii."	Áshịị	iizee
I	it	now	doctor	to him	I speak	And then	medicine

áyiił'ịị'íí	Abáachii	doo	nzhógo	yégósị'íí
she makes it one who	Apache	not	well	she knows it one who

yidóoł	áyiiłníí,	"Éí	haskịịyịịzháá	ndé'ee	sidá'íí
doctor	she tells him	that	little old man	there	he sits one who

miik'éé	nchaa	shịị	k'e' diinii,"	áyiiłníí.
his relatives	they swell	and	they hurt	she says

Translation: A little old man, his feet swollen and hurting, went to the hospital. At the hospital the nurse asked him, "What ails you, Grandpa?" The old man replied, "My feet are swollen and they hurt." The nurse said, "All right, Grandpa, I'll tell the doctor." The nurse, who didn't speak Apache well, said to the doctor, "That little old man sitting over there has swollen relatives and they hurt."

▼ ▼ ▼ ▼

The following tongue-twister plays upon the sibilant characteristics of the sounds represented by *ł*, *sh*, *tł*, and *tł'*, all in combination with the vowel *ii*. Rapid recitation of this cascade of sound guarantees native laughter. There is a closely-related Navajo version.

Dził	**łikishííshį́į**	**haskįįyį́į**	**łikishíí**	**łį́į**	**łikishíí**
mountain	spotted one from	man	spotted one	horse	spotted one

namiiyégo	**mił**	**ííłtłishgo**	**mił**	**náásmąsgo**
he riding it	with him	it stumbled	with him	it rolled

áshíí	**náátłish**	**miigwo**	**díítł'ish.**
and then	he fell off	his knee	he bruised

Translation: A spotted man from a spotted mountain was riding along on a spotted horse. The horse stumbled and rolled with him and he fell off, bruising his knee.

▼ ▼ ▼ ▼

This piece of humor uses the homophonic (same sound) properties of *nóoshch'ii'yé miikah* (among the pinyons) and *ch'íidn miika'yé* (among the spirits, ghosts), with the added implication that grandmothers do not hear well, to make the pun. There is a Navajo version of close similarity which uses the words *neeshch'íítah* (among the pinyons) and *ch'į́idiitah* (among the spirits) to the same purpose.

Ishkiiyį́įzháá	**miichóó**	**áyiiłníí,**	**"Ha'go**	**nóoshch'íí'yé**
a small boy	his grandmother	he says to her	when	to pinyons

miikah	**dínyá?"**
among them	you are going

"Oo,	**shiiyii'íí,**	**ch'íidn**	**miika'yé**	**doo**	**naashá**	**hásht'íí."**
oh	my son	spirits, ghosts	among to	not	I walk about	I want

Translation: A small boy said to his grandmother, "When are you going to pick pinyons?" "Oh, My Son (she replied), I don't want to walk among the spirits."

Taboos

▼▼▼▼

Shǫǫdii	ts'iyiiłtségo	dá'yá'déé	ntǫǫ'é	ts'idiits'e
coyote	seeing it	everything	it is bad	hearing it

doodago	ntǫǫ'é'íí.	Ts'iiłtsé	shíí	shǫǫdii	ts'iiłts'ego
or	it is bad one	one who sees him	and	coyote	one who hears him

gé	miich'į	késhdiidlii	kádńdín	mee.	Késhdiidliigo
just	him to	you pray	pollen	it with.	if you pray

ntǫǫ'é	nówoch'įgo	áyiilé.
evil	away	he makes it

Translation: It is bad to see or hear a coyote anywhere. If you should see or hear a coyote, pray to Him (the Jicarilla deity) with an offering of pollen. Praying to Him will make the evil go away.

▼▼▼▼

Nagoołkįįhgo	shíí	idiłch'iłgo	łíí	doo	goł
When it is raining	and	there is lightning	horse	not	with it

hádiikaaz	da.	Idiłch'iłgo	goyiłhé
it runs about	not	the lightning	it will kill one

Translation: Don't ride a horse when it is raining and there is lightning. The lightning will kill you.

▼▼▼▼

Maashjé'	doo	nadiłtsee	da.	Łe'	nadzistseego
spider	not	kill it	not.	one	if one kills it

áshdiinii'íí,	"Shiichóó	má	yéłhíí,"	ch'idiinii
what one says	my grandmother	her for	I killed it	one says

Translation: Do not kill a spider. If you should kill one you must say, "I killed it for my grandmother."

116

▼ ▼ ▼ ▼

Gwii'	naasyá'yé	doo	miikáá'	nach'igháِ	da.
snake	it went where	not	it upon	one walks	not

Gojádii	niigai	daach'inii.
one's leg	it will start hurting	they say

Translation: Do not walk upon a snake's track. They say that your leg will start to hurt.

▼ ▼ ▼ ▼

Dá'yá'déé	gwii'	mee	áyaa'íí	doo	mee	nach'igháِ,
everything	snake	it with	it is made one	not	it with	one walks

ntǫ́ǫ́'é	ééyaa.
it is bad	because

Translation: It is bad to walk around wearing anything made from a snake.

▼ ▼ ▼ ▼

Chíníí	shį́į́	mósha	doo	naméch'iɫchii	da.	Ha'ńda ga
dog	and	cat	not	one buys it	not	someone

yiiɫkeegonáِ	nzhǫ́,	doodago	ga	daatsei	shį́į́
one gives it	it is good	if not	one	it will die	and

wó'	iighai.
away	it goes

Translation: Don't buy a dog or a cat. It is fine if somone gives one to you, otherwise it will either die or run away.

▼ ▼ ▼ ▼

Sǫǫs	doo	ch'ólchíí	da.	Sǫǫs*	ga	haagháí.
star(s)	not	one points	not.	wart(s)	one	it will appear upon

Translation: Don't point at stars. You will get warts.

*Sǫǫs means both *star(s)* and *wart(s)*.

117

Appendix 2 ◀◀◀◀

Seasons

spring — dąą
summer — shíí
fall — dą́ą́k'ee
winter — hai

Months

January — Koghanee (at home; by the fire)
February — Itsáízháá (small eagles)
March — Miinii Ch'íidn (spirit faces)
April — It'ą́ą́náchiilii (small leaves)
May — It'ą́ą́nátso (big leaves)
June — Hóniiyo (Spanish, *junio)*
July — Gáadolo (Spanish, *julio)*
August — Awóoshdo (Spanish, *agosto)*
September — Gojíiya (Spanish, *cuchillo?)*
October — It'ą́ą́nshch'ilíí (curled leaves)
November — Kajee biłdaa'idą́ (turkey feast)
December — Ochoweda (n.a.)

Days of the Week

Monday — Na'iidziijį́í (work day)
Tuesday — Máałdis (Spanish, *martes)*
Wednesday — Ich'énádzoł
   (exact meaning unknown)
Thursday — Ich'énedzoo
   (exact meaning unknown)
Friday — Ich'é (entrails)
Saturday — Lasóon (English, *ration)*
Sunday — Doona'iidziijį́í (day of no work)

Foods

apples — mansáana (Spanish, *manzana)*
banana — goshk'an
beans — naa'oléé
bread — łeet'áan
butter — mandagíiya (Spanish, *mantequilla)*
cheese — iibe' nesdǫ'íí
chili — jíilii (Sp., *chili)*
coffee — gahée (Sp., *café)*
cookies — łeet'áan liką'íí
corn — naadą́'
eggs — iyezhii
fat, lard — ik'a
fish — łógee
flour — ik'an
fry bread — ts'íłiłii
meat — itsįį
melon — k'ech'iyą́'éé
milk — iibe'
mush — adóolii
orange — ch'ił łitso'íí
pear — béela (Sp., *pera)*
pop — kólichíí'íí
potatoes — bába (Sp., *papa)*
pumpkin — naayizéé
rice — alóos (Sp., *arroz)*
salt — íshǫǫsh
squash — naayizéé
stew — káził
tea — dééh (Sp., *té)*
sugar — asóokala (Sp., *azúcar)*
tomatoes — domáadii (Sp., *tomate)*
vegetables — neest'áan
watermelon — chandíiya (Sp., *sandía)*

Kinship

The following terms are written with the possessive pronoun *shii-*, for example, *shiichóó,* my grandmother:

grandmother — shiichóó
grandfather — shiitsóóyéé
grandson, grandaughter — shiitsóóyíí
mother — shii'máá
father — shiika'éé
daughter — shiizhách'į'íí
son — shiiyii'íí
older sister — shiidádéé
younger sister — shiishdázha
older brother — shiiną'áá
younger brother — shiishdázha
aunt — shiibéch'éé
uncle — shiidą'áá
niece — shiizhách'į'íí
nephew — shiiyii'íí
cousin — shiizeedń
wife — shii'á, shii'iisdzáníí
husband — shiihaskįįyíí
in-laws — shii'iyé
daughter-in-law and son-in-law — shadaaníí
father-in-law and mother-in-law —
    shiizháá'á

Animals (native fauna)

animals — aliimáał
antelope — da'aghaadii
bear — shash
beaver — cháá
bobcat — ndói
buffalo — iyánéé
cat — mósha
cow — bóó
cottontail — gałbáyéé
coyote — shǫǫdii, sitł'idéen

deer — bįį
dog — chíníí
elk — dzées
fish — łógee
frog — ch'ałdéé
goat — jíiva
gopher — dlǫ'
horned toad — ma'iishǫ'íí dich'ich'éé
horse — łíí
jack rabbit — gahtso
lamb — dibé miizháá
lizard — ma'iishǫ'íí
mountain goat — dibé dził
mountain lion — ndói
mouse — ma'íísts'ǫsdéé
mule — ja'áá
pig — ní'gotł'its'íí
porcupine — ts'ó
prairie dog — dlǫ'
rattlesnake — gwii' bitséégháléé
sheep — dibé
skunk — k'élích'éé
snake — gwii'
squirrel — naojiłgai
turtle — ts'óskeeł
wolf — ba'iitso

bird(s) — tsidéé
buzzard — t'á'jázhéé
chicken — ǫǫ́haiyee
crane — t'áałbai
crow — gáagee
duck — naał'ełéé
eagle — itsá
hawk — itséłtsoíí
hummingbird — ilatsoíí
magpie — ą'ai
meadowlark — tł'eshwózhíí
owl — yíí'yee
robin — gochish
turkey — kajee
woodpecker — chishkałdéé

bug(s) — gó'yee
bee — ts'ósdá
black ant — gódashchídéé lizhįį'íí
butterfly — maashlógee
cricket — gwii'ts'inéé
fly — ts'ííyee
grasshopper — maashchagéé
horsefly — łįįts'ííyee
mosquito — dzaats'ózéé
red ant — gódashchídéé łichíí'íí
spider — maashjé'

Trees and Plants (native flora)

alder — k'ish
apple — mansáana
aspen — it'ą́ązháá
blue spruce — nóoshzhaa
cedar — kałdéé
cottonwood — t'ǫǫs
fir — jǫ'oł
juniper — gáh
leaves — it'ą́ą́
oak — chóshch'ilii
pear — béela
pine tree — nóoshchii
pinyon nut — nóoshch'íí
pinyon pine — izeełchíí
pitch — jee
sumac — k'įį
willow — k'ai'

berry — dzé
cactus — wozhéé
cattail — tł'okakeeł
chili — jíilii
corn — naadą́'
flower — tł'ozháá
gooseberry — dałwozhee
grass — tł'oh
sagebrush — ts'e

squash — naayizéé
sunflower — iláka'its'éé
wheat — tł'onaadą́'
yucca — ich'ą́ą́wosh

Shapes, Sizes, and Textures

bent — diigį́į́
big — ntsaa
braided — hishbish
circular — sibąs
crooked — diigis
curly — hishdlosh
deep — diką́
dull — doo deeníí da
flat, wide — nkeeł
fuzzy — ditł'ó
glassy — k'éts'iłii
greasy — ik'a dá małánéé
hard — ntł'is
having holes, perforated — ghá'gosh'áan
long — ndees
rocky — tsé dáłánéé
rough — dich'ísh
rubbery — nadiits'ǫǫs
shallow — kóh áłch'ííshdéé
sharp — deeníí
skinny — dik'ą́ą́né
slippery, smooth — diłkǫǫh
small — áłts'íísdé
soupy — gé kóh át'é
strong — naałwo
swollen — nchaa
thick — diką́
tough — diits'id
twisted — iłk'énásgis
woven — histł'ól

Appendix 3 ◀ ◀ ◀ ◀

Verb Paradigms

The verbs presented throughout this course have been primarily displayed in the first three persons singular. The paradigms appearing below are samples to provide you with an insight into the formation of the three persons of the dual and distributive plural, as well. The designations in parentheses denote simple present or past tense. Keep in mind that present tense is also often used to express future action and that the enclitic *ńt'éé* may be used with present tense (impefective) verbs to render an imperfective past, i.e., *was* or *used to*.

To go, to start going (present)	**To go and return (past)**
Singular	**Singular**
1st déya	naséyá
2nd dínyá	nasínyá
3rd deeyá (deesyá)	naasyá
Dual	**Dual**
1st diit'ásh	nashiit'ásh
2nd dá'ásh	nasha'ásh
3rd deesh'ásh	naash'ásh
Distributive Plural	**Distributive Plural**
1st díikai	nasiikai
2nd dákai	nasakai
3rd deeskai	naaskai

To work (present)

Singular

1st	na'iisii
2nd	na'íízii
3rd	na'iizii

Dual

1st	na'iidzii
2nd	na'azii
3rd	na'iizii

Distributive Plural

1st	nada'iidzii
2nd	nada'azii
3rd	nada'iizii

To work (past)

Singular

1st	na'sézii
2nd	na'sínzii
3rd	na'iiszii

Dual

1st	na'siidzii
2nd	na'sasii
3rd	na'iiszii

Distributive Plural

1st	nada'siidzii
2nd	nada'sasii
3rd	nada'iiszii

To want (present)

Singular

1st	hásht'íí
2nd	hánt'íí
3rd	yííkát'íí

Dual

1st	háat'íí
2nd	hát'íí
3rd	yííkát'íí

Distributive Plural

1st	hádaat'íí
2nd	hádát'íí
3rd	yííkádaat'íí

To walk about (present)

Singular

1st	naashá
2nd	nandá
3rd	naaghá

Dual

1st	naat'aash
2nd	na'aash
3rd	naa'aash

Distributive Plural

1st	naakai
2nd	nákai
3rd	naakai

To be (present)

Singular
1st	nishłį́į́
2nd	ńłį́į́
3rd	nilį́į́

Dual
1st	ndlį́į́
2nd	nahłį́į́
3rd	nilį́į́

Distributive Plural
1st	daandlį́į́
2nd	daanahłį́į́
3rd	daanilį́į́

To understand it (present)

Singular
diists'e
diints'e
yidiits'e

Dual
diits'e
daats'e
yidiits'e

Distributive Plural
daadiits'e
daadaats'e
daayidiits'e

To see it (past)

Singular
1st	heełtsą́
2nd	hiinłtsą́
3rd	yiiłtsą́

Dual
1st	hiiltsą́
2nd	haałtsą́
3rd	yiiłtsą́

Distributive Plural
1st	daahiiltsą́
2nd	daahaałtsą́
3rd	daayiiłtsą́

To buy it (present)

Singular
naméshchii
naménłchii
nayéłchii

Dual
naméełchii
namélchii
nayéłchii

Distributive Plural
naméedaałchii
namédaałchii
nayédaałchii

Appendix 4 ◀◀◀◀

Notes on Some Linguistic Aspects of Jicarilla Apache

A fundamental objective of this course is to establish a firm working knowledge of the first three persons singular of a great number of verbs persistently and recurrently used by the Jicarilla Apache. In this book the first three persons singular of each verb are given in present and past tenses. It is to be noted that the present tense of Jicarilla Apache verbs is very frequently used to express future action.

The verbs in this course are in forms relating primarily to action in progress, expressions of future action, and completed action, largely and generally speaking, and are therefore considered present, future and past tense for the sake of simplicity. In this, a beginning course in language so different from English, simplicity is paramount to the attainment of a grasp of material that will make further, more detailed inquiry possible. For such study I refer the student to the work of Harry Hoijer on the Apachean verb in the *International Journal of American Linguistics* (IJAL: Parts I-V, 1945-49).

It is not within the scope of this basic course to explore in detail the intricacies of the Apachean verb. In the deeper recesses of Apachean linguistics the terms *aspect* and *mode* are used for the verb in relation to completion of action, action in progress, habituality of action, repetition of action, and so forth. The Apachean verb, in general, often consists of various modifiers, subject and object pronouns, and, in its stem, a verbal concept or idea, so that the verb is in itself a complete sentence whose elements are in a fixed order.

The explanations following the dialogs of each unit, in additon to supplying detailed discussion of dialog items, also contain frequent references to the related linguistics of the Apachean languages mentioned in the Introduction. These expositions will be of interest to speakers of these languages, to students of Athabascan languages and to language *aficionados* at large.

Jicarilla Apache syntax (structural pattern) is markedly dissimilar to English syntax. The following personal statement, with interlinear word-for-word translation, will provide an insight into the typical structure and other stylistic characteristics of Jicarilla Apache discourse:

1. **Shíí** **Rita** **shíízhii.** **Lósii'yé** **shii'deeshchíí** **shíí** **á'ee**
   I   Rita   my name   Dulce at   I was born   and   there

2. **néésai.** **Shiika'éé** **na'iizii'íí** **nahiikéyaa'íí** **miiná'iisdzo'íí**
   I grew up   my father   his work   our land   its boundaries

3. **éí** **yaa** **shishíí.** **Shii'máá** **éí** **gé** **koghạ'yé** **sidá**
   they them for he cared   my mother   she   just   home at   she sits

4. **nahaa** **daashishíí.** **Shiidádéé** **naakii.** **Dáłaa'é** **éí**
   us for   she cared   my older sisters two   one   she

5. **édįį.** **Dáłaa'é** **éí** **dá aada'é** **miighạ.** **Shiishdázha**
   she is gone one   she   far away   her home   my younger sisters

6. **dáłánéé.** **Ałtsọ** **nada'iizii.** **Łe'** **dá** **á'ee** **Lósii'ee**
   many   they all   they work   some   just   there   Dulce at

7. **daamighạ.** **Isgwéela'yé** **naséyá,** **éí** **Lósii'ee**
   their separate homes school to   I went   it   Dulce at

8. **naséyá** **dá** **ánsts'íísédạ́.** **Łe'gó** **Santa Fe'yé** **dáłaa'é**
   I went   quite I am small when   and then   Santa Fe at   one

9. **hai** **shee** **goslíí** **á'ee.** **Łe'gó** **Ináaso'yé** **éí** **kái'ii**
   winter me with it became there   and then   Ignacio at   it   three

10. **hai** **shee** **goslíí.** **Dá** **á'ee** **égóółdįį.** **Áshíí** **ikéé'go**
    winters me with it became just there I finished   and then   later

11. **Dziłntsaa'yé** **iizee** **áyiił'íí** **má** **naséyá,** **áshíí**
    mountain big at   medicine she makes it it for I went   and then

12. **ikéé'go** **á'ee** **da'iijołyé** **na'sézii.** **Áshíí** **shiihaskįiyíí**
    later   there   everywhere   I worked   and then   my husband

13. **goslíígo** **shii'łchíníí** **gosts'idii,** **ch'ekéé** **díí'ii** **shíí** **diidé kái'ii.**
    he became when my children   seven   girl(s)   four   and   boy(s) three

125

Free Translation

My name is Rita. I was born and grew up in Dulce, New Mexico. My father worked to take care of our land. My mother stayed home and took care of all of us. I had two older sisters. One of them is deceased. The other lives far from here. I have many younger sisters. They all work. Some of them live in Dulce. When I was a youngster I went to school in Dulce. Then I lived for a year in Santa Fe. Later I lived for three years in Ignacio, Colorado. I left there and went to Albuquerque to study nursing and later worked there in several places. Then I married and now have four daughters and three sons.

Note some of the following interesting syntactical and other distinctions between Jicarilla Apache and English:

1. The verb comes at the end of the sentence.

2. Subject and possessive pronouns (the latter, in written form, are prefixed to the noun) are generally differentiated by tone (Line 1, shíí — *I,* shii — *my*).

3. Positional and directional prepositions are represented by enclitics that follow, rather than precede (as in English), place designations (Line 1, Losii'yé — *Dulce at, Dulce to*).

4. A relatival enclitic is used to particularize verbs and nouns (Line 2, na'iizii — *he works,* na'iizii'íí — *he is the one who works, his work*; nahiikéyaa — *our land,* nahiikéyaa'íí — *our particular land*).

5. Prepositions are postpounded to personal pronouns, unlike English in which prepositions are prepounded, or precede, personal pronouns (Line 3, yaa shishíí — *them for he cared*, where *y-* means *him, her, them* and *-aa* signifies *for.*

6. There are few noun plural forms in Jicarilla Apache. One form usually serves to render both singular and plural (Line 4, shiidádéé — *my younger sister, my younger sisters*).

7. Adjectives regularly follow nouns (Lines 5 and 6, shiishdázha dáłánéé — *my sisters many*).

8. Gender is not expressed in 3rd person pronoun forms (Line 5, miigha — *his home, her home*). Context determines which gender is meant.

9. Both singular and dual 3rd person possessive pronouns are represented by the same element, *mii-*, which precedes the noun and can indicate one, as well as two, possessors (Line 5, miigha — *his, her, their (two) home(s)*.

10. Distributive plural elements (*-da-* or *-daa-*) are prefixed to, or infixed within, verbs or nouns (Lines 6 and 7, nada'iizii — *they work (more than two);* daamiigha — *their homes, their individual homes*).

11. There are no articles in Jicarilla Apache (Line 11, *Dzihtsaa,* in this case a Jicarilla Apache place name for Albuquerque, New Mexico, may be translated as *big mountain, the big mountain,* or *a big mountain*).

Index ◀◀◀◀

This English–Jicarilla Apache index provides a general reference to the vocabulary, phraseology, and grammatical concepts displayed in lesson units 1–21, and in some of the appendices. In the absence of infinitive verb forms in Jicarilla Apache, verbs are presented, for the most part, in the first person singular, present as well as past tenses. Thus, the verb *work* appears as *na'iisii* (I work, I am working), and *worked* as *na'sézii* (I worked), each item followed by a page number. Kinship and anatomical terms are listed with prefixed first person possessive pronouns: mother — *shii'máá* (my mother); hand — *shííla* (my hand).

basket — íseezis, 13
be — nishłį́į́, 32
beans — naa'oléé, 118
bear — shash, 119
beautiful — gooyéé, 2
beautiful — nzhǫ́, 4, 110
beaver — ch33, 119
because, on account of — íí yąą, 49
bed — ts'ísk'eh, 92
bee — ts'ósdá, 120
begin — nkee gózhísh, 80
behind — miide'shį́į́, 90
bent — diigį́į́, 120
berry — dzé, 120
big — ntsaa, 20
bird — tsidéé, 119
bitter — ńk'ǫsh, 57
black — łizhįį, 62
black ant — gódashchídéé łizhįį'íí, 120
blanket — biilii, 92
blow — deesyoł, 77
blue (green) — daatł'ish, 62
blue spruce — nóoshzhaa, 120
bobcat — ndóí, 119
boil it — hishbésh, 100
boiled it — séłbésh, 100
boiled — shiibéésh, 28
book — naałtsoozii, 64
born — shii'deeshchį́į́, 81
both — dáłínt'an, 84
bought — naméshéłchii, 46
bracelet — látsínéé, 45
braided — hishbish, 120
bread — łeet'áan, 118
broom — begozhǫ́'íí, 70
brown — dinishzhį, 62
buffalo — iyánéé, 119
bug — gó'yee, 120
build — ágoshłé, 95
building — kįį, 9, 10
built — ágoshłaa, 95
built a fire — de'dééłjéé, 56

bumpy — godiwoł, 55
burned — ńdlii, 57
but — énda, 9, 10
butter — mandagíiya, 118
butterfly — maashlógee, 120
buy — naméshchii, 44
buzzard — t'á'jázhéé, 119
by it — miibąąch'į, 60
by means of it — mee, yee, 34, 36

C

cactus — wozhéé, 120
candy — lósii, 17
cane — gish, 90
car battery — bííł miijéé, 44, 45
car — bííł, 9, 11
carpenter — kįį áyiił'į́'íí, 31
cat — mósha, 119
catch cold — dikosdéé she'ńłde, 49
cattail — tł'okakeeł, 120
cedar — kałdéé, 120
cent — sindáo, 44
chair — k'edahiisdáíí, 90
cheese — iibe' nesdǫ'íí, 118
chest — shiijé', 51
chicken — ǫ́ǫhaiyee, 119
children — íłchíń, 27
chili — jíilii, 118
cigarette — nát'ohdii, 90
circular — sibąs, 120
clay pot — ísee goshtł'ish, 12
clear sky — k'os édįį, 77
close (v) — Ną'hęę ńkįį, 68
closer — áháánégo, 95
clothes, dress — é, 44
cloudy — k'os, 77
coffee — gahée, 118
cold (illness) — dikosdéé, 49
cold (object) — sik'as, 28
cold (weather) — goosk'as, 1, 2
cold — hishdló, 51
cold — shił goosk'as, 24

129

come in — ye' iindééh, 24
content — shił gohwii, 73
cook *(n)* — dáan áyiił'íí'íí, 30
cook *(v)* — dáan áyiił'íí, 31
cookies — łeet'áan łika'íí, 118
corn meal mush — adóolii, 22
corn — naadá', 118, 120
corpulent — dá łik'aa'é, 109
correct — éíłt'áo, 19
costs — íílíí, 44, 45
cottontail — gałbáyéé, 119
cottonwood — t'ǫǫs, 120
cough *(v)* — diskos, 51
country — kéyaa, 74
cousin — shiizeedń, 119
cow — bóó, 119
coyote — shǫǫdii, sitł'idéen, 119
crane — t'áałbai, 119
crayons — me'iichíshíí, 70
cricket — gwii'ts'inéé, 120
cried — hiicha, 107
crooked — diigis, 120
crow — gáagee, 62, 119
cry — hishcha, 107
cupboard — kéłts'ei miighą, 91
curly — hishdlosh, 120
cut — shégish, 24

D

damp — gé godiit'ó, 77
dance — diishdlo, 94
danced — déédlo, 94
daughter — shiizhách'į'íí, 119
daughter-in-law and son-in-law —
    shadaaníí, 119
December — Ochoweda, 118
deep — diką, 120
deer — bįį, 58, 119
die — daastsą, 103
difficult for me — ch'éh ásh'íí, 3, 4
dish — kéłts'ei, 91
do — ásh'íí, 15

doctor — yidóoł, 32
does not exist — édįį, 34, 35
dog — chíníí, 119
dollar — béeso, 44
down there — hayaach'į, 58, 59
drank — éédlą, 65
drink (it, something) — hishdlą, 65, 66
drink — ishdlą, 65, 66
drive — naashło, 83
drove nasélo, 83
drunk — shił goosdo, 73
duck — naał'ełéé, 119
Dulce, New Mexico — Lósii, 1
dull — doo deeníí da, 120
during the day — jíígo, 56
díí'íí — this one, 52

E

eagle — itsá, 119
ear — shiijaa, 51
earrings — jaatł'ół, 45
east — sháha'áí, 39, 40
eat (it, something) — hishą, 66
eat — ishą, 66
egg — iyezhii, 118
elk — dzées, 119
ends — égóósdįį, 80
English — Mągáanii, 6
everything — dá'yá'déé, 109
everywhere — dá ałtsǫ'yé, dá ha'yé,
    dá'iijoołyé, 109
exists, they exist — góníí, 20
expensive — íílíí, 44, 45
eye — shiidáá, 51

F

fall (season) — dą́ą́k'ee, 118
far — dá aada'é, 19
farther — dá adaahégo, 95
fat, lard — ik'a, 118
father — shiika'éé, 119
father-in-law and mother-in-law —

shiizháá'á, 119

feast — kéesda, 30

February — Itsáízháá, 118

fine with me — doo shił ási, 49

fir — jo'oł, 120

fire — ko, 16

firewood — chish, 14

fish — łógee, 118

fishing pole — łogee mehadloo'íí, 90

fits (v) — shiik'eh, 46

five dollars — ashdle' béeso, 34

fix — nzhógo áshłé, 107

fixed — nzhógo áshłaa, 107

flat, wide — nkeeł, 120

flour — ik'an, 118

flower — tł'ozháá, 120

fly — ts'ííyee, 120

food — dáan, 22

foot — shiikee, 51

for a long time, a long time ago —
    dałk'iidá, 98

for it — mííká, 86

for it, after it — há, 92

for me — shá, 44, 45

for the purpose of — íí yąą, 61

for whom — ha'ń yá, 61

for you — ná, 44, 45

for, in exchange for — bik'édéé, 34

forgot it — ménásisdee, 98

found — náheełtsá, 69

found him, her, it (he, she) — náyiiłtsá, 69

four days ago — díí'ii yiskądá, 104

Friday — Ich'é, 118

fried (v) — séłt'é, 101

friend — shiich'oonii, 17

frog — ch'ałdéé, 119

from — shíí, 1,2

from here — ii'eeshíí, 39

frosty — shóh, 77

fry — hist'ees, 101

fry bread — ts'ííłiłii, 118

frying pan — mets'iiłt'eesíí, 70

funny — ma'goołkąą, 47

fuzzy — ditł'ó, 120

G

gasoline — bííł miikoo, 9

get up — nádiishdééh, 86

get — nádiistsós, 93

give — sha ń'ai, 64

glassy — k'éts'iłii, 120

go away — nówoch'į nandá, 37

go — déyá, 1, 9

goat — jíiva, 119

good — hooyéé, nzhó, 1, 3

gooseberry — dałwozhee, 120

gopher — dló', 119

got it — nádeełtsoos, 92, 93

got up — nádiisdzá, 86

grandfather — shiitsóóyéé, 119

grandmother — shiichóó, 119

grandson, grandaughter — shiitsóóyíí, 119

grass — tł'oh, 120

grasshopper — maashchagéé, 120

gray — łibá, 62

greasy — ik'a dá małánéé, 120

grew up — néésai, 82

H

hailing — iloo naałkiįh, 77

hairy — miitsii dáłánéé, 62

hand — shííla, 24

happy — shił gózhó, 73

hard — ntł'is, 120

hat — ch'ał, 44

hate — mee diishnii, 90

have lived — shee goslíí, 98

have — see Unit 3 Dialog, p.11, no. 11

having holes, perforated — ghá'gosh'áan,
    120

hawk — itséłtsoíí, 119

he — bíí, áń, 8

head — shiitsii, 51

hear — diists'e, 3, 4

lay down — nékį́į́, 18
lazy — shił góóyé'é, 73
leader — nant'áan, 32
learn it — méoniisįį, 3, 4
learned it — méosésįį, 6
leaves — it'ą́ą́, 120
leg — shiijádii, 51
let's (the two of us) go — diit'ash, 34
let's build a fire — de'ńljee, 49
lie *(n)* — naach'á, 52
lie *(v)* — naashch'á, 52
lie down —sékį́į́, 18
light (weight) — ászóólé, 28
lightning — idiłch'ił, 77
like it (food, drink) — shił łiką, 17
like it (other than food) — shił gooyéé, 1, 17
listen — hííyésts'ą́, 95
listened — hííyéółts'ą́, 95
live *(v)* — shee goslį́į́, 98, 99
lizard — ma'iishǫ'íí, 119
loaf *(v)* — gé ásht'įį, 88
lonely — dá shííná sédá, 90
long — ndees, 120
look — dín'íį, 62
look at — nésh'íį, 100
look for — há nanshká, 69
love — nkásht'íį, 90
lying in position — siłtsoos, 92

M

ma gózhǫ́ — good natured, 110
made — ágoshłaa, 12, 95
made of — mee áyaa, 96
magpie — ą'ai, 119
make — ágoshłé, áshłé, 12
man — haskįįyíí, 54
many — dáłánéé, 20
March — Miinii Ch'íidn, 118
May — It'ą́ą́nátso, 118
meadowlark — tł'eshwózhíí, 119
mean — dá hashké'é, 109
meat — itsįį, 118

medicine man — haskįįyíí gokaałii, 32
medicine — iizee, 7
melancholy — shił gótǫ́ǫ́'é, 73
melon — k'ech'iyą́'éé, 118
melt — nááłhį́į́h, 36
Mescalero Apache — Nadaíin, 7
Mescalero reservation — Nadaíin
    miikéyaa, 27
milk — iibe', 118
mind *(n)* — míínii, 72
Monday — Na'iidziijį́į́, 118
money — zháał, 22, 34, 38
moon — tł'é'na'áí, 84
morning — nłdą́'go, 84
mosquito — dzaats'ózéé, 120
mother — shii'máá, 119
mountain(s) — dził, 20
mountain lion — ndóí, 119
mountain sheep — dibé dził, 58, 59
mouse — ma'íísts'ǫsdéé, 119
mouth — shiize', 51
Mr. — haskįįyíí, 54
much — dáłánéé, 44
much, a lot — łą́o, 44
mud — goshtł'ish, 54
muddy — goshtł'ish, 55
mule — ja'áá, 119
mush — adóolii, 118
my — shii-, 11

N

Navajo reservation — Inłt'ánéé miikéyaa,
    74
Navajo — Inłt'ánéé, 6
nearby — áháánéé, 41
nephew — shiiyii'íį, 119
next month — nádeezigo, 17
nice — dá hooyéé, 4, 5
nice — hooyéé, dá gooyéé, 4, 5
nicely — nzhǫ́go, 2
niece — shiizhách'į'íį, 119
night — tł'é'go, 84

no — dooda, 3, 4
noon — iłních'i'n'ágo, 84
north — náakosii, 39
nose — shiichísh, 51
not far — doo aada da, 9, 10
November — Kajee Biłdaa'idá, 118
now — dákoo, 9
nurse — iizee áyił'íí'íí, 32

O

o.k. — doo ásį, 54
oak tree — chóshch'ilii, 58, 59, 120
October — It'áánshch'ilíí, 118
oil — bííł miik'a, 44
older brother — shiina'áá, 119
older sister — shiidádéé, 119
on foot, walking — dá nii', 86, 87
on it, on top of it — miikáá'yé, 58, 59
on Saturday — Lasóongo, 9
on the floor, ground — nii'yé, 92
once — dáła'éédii, 109
once in a while — dá nááná ha'go, 109
open the door — kwe' ńkįį, 68
orange — ch'ił łitso'íí, 118
other — łe', 109
ouch — aíí, 19
our (two) — nahii-, 11
our (more than two) — danahii-, 11
outside — tł'ó'yé, 49
over there — ndé'ee, ndééch'į, ách'į, 9, 10
owl — yíí'yee, 119

P

Pagosa — Bawóoso, 52
paid — ná'nílá, 74
paint — hishdleesh, 82
painted — shédléésh, 82
paper — naałtsoozii, 93
part (a little) of it — dá'áłts'íísdégo, 109
pay, will pay — ná'nshłé, 74
pear — béela, 118
pencil — mek'e'iilchíí, 70

people — diidé, 22
pig — ní'gotł'its'íí, 119
pine tree — nóoshchii, 58, 59, 120
pinyon nut — nóoshch'íí, 120
pinyon pine — izeełchíí, 120
pitch — jee, 120
plant (v) — k'ediishłé, 106
planted — k'edéélá, 106
play — naashdéé, 88
played — nasédéé, 89
pleasant — dá gooyéé, 20
porcupine — ts'ó, 119
pot — ísee, 64
potatoes — bába, 118
pow-wow — godasyé, 82
prairie dog — dló', 119
pregnant — hiiłtsá, 60
probably — shíí, 92
pumpkin — naayizéé, 118

Q

quite — dá, 2

R

rabbit — gah, 58, 119
rain (v) — nagoołkįįh, 36
ran — ídénééká, 94
rattlesnake — gwii' bitséégháléé, 119
read — óshkai, 94
read (past tense) — óołkai, 94
really — doo ńdaadé, 56
red — łichíí, 62
red ant — gódashchídéé łichíí'íí, 120
reliable — ma ch'óolíí, 72
remember it — ménáshnii, 98
repeat it — ánáá dńíí, 32
return — nádiishdááł, 75
returned — nánsdzá, 74
rice — alóos, 118
ride (v) — naashiiyégo, 101
ridiculous — gé ntóó'é, 57
ring — la'níích'éé, 48

river — kónlíí, 12
road — ííkin, 54
robin — gochish, 119
rock — tsé, 58, 59
rocky — tsé dáłánéé, 120
rode — naasiisyíí, 101
rope — tł'ół, 78, 88
rough — dich'ísh, 120
round — łiijooł, 28
rubbery — nadiits'ǫǫs, 120
run — hiskas, 94
run — íídéenshká, 94, 95

S

sagebrush — ts'e, 58, 59
salt — íshǫǫsh, 118
San Carlos Apache — Łeeshchíí, 7
sand — séí, 54
sandy — séí, 55
sang — ha'déé'á, 83
Saturday — Lasóon, 118
saw (n) — iik'aashíí, 70
saw it — heełtsá, 39
school bus — bííl iłchíń naiyé'íí, 86
school — isgwéela, 3, 4
scram — nówoch'į, 37
secretary — segidéeł, 32
see it — hish'íí, 58
seek — há nanshká, 69
sell — -ch'į naméshchii, 46
September — Gojíiya, 118
set (sun) — shá'íí'á, 42
shallow — kóh áłch'ííshdéé, 120
sharp — deeníí, 120
she — bíí, áń, 120
shear (sheep) — hiishé, 18
sheared — héshé, 18
sheep — dibé, 119
shine (stars) — k'éts'iłii, 42
short — gé áłts'íísdé, 109
shoulder — shiiwos, 51
shy — yá nsįį, 73

sick — dinshnii, 49
sing — ha'dish'éí, 83
sit — sédá, 88
skinny — dik'ą́ą́né, 120
skunk — k'élích'éé, 119
sleep — iishhásh, 17
sleepy — bił nsįį, 51
slender — gé dik'ą́ą́né, 109
slept — eełhaash, 18
slippery (road) — godiłkǫǫh, 37
slippery — diłkǫǫh, 120
small — áłts'íísdé, 120
smells — gołchį, 101
smooth — diłkǫǫh, 120
snake — gwii', 119
snow — zas, 20
snowing — zas nagoołkįįh, 77
soda pop — kólichíí'íí, 36
sold — -ch'į nameshéłchii, 46
some — łe', 9, 10
son — shiiyii'íí, 119
songs — ha'dii'éí, miiyin, 95
soon — dák'adéé, 15
soupy — gé kóh át'é, 120
sour — ńk'ǫǫsh, 57
south — shádii'áí, 39
Spanish — Naakaiiyéé, 25
speak it — yáshkii, 25
spend the night — shee yiiłkái, 50
spent the night — shee yiiská, 49
spider — maashjé', 120
spoiled — ńłdzii, 57
spring — dąą, 118
squash — naayizéé, 118
squirrel — naojiłgai, 119
stand — sézįį, 86, 87
start — nkee, 80
stew — káził, 118
stick — chish, 90
stomach — shiibii, 51
store — kįį, 9
strong — naałwo, 120

student — ółkai'íí, 71
stupid — doo góyá, 73
sugar — asóokala, 118
sumac — k'įį, 120
summer — shį́į́, 118
Sunday — Doona'iidziijį́í, 118
sunflower — iláka'its'éé, 120
sunrise — ha'íí'ágo, 84
sunset — shá'íí'ágo, 84
swam — na'sétkó, 83
sweet — łika, 57
swim — na'ishkógo, 83
swollen — nchaa, 120

T

table — miiká'dahch'iyá'íí, 90
take — nį̣ diish'ash, 36
talk — yáshkii, 25, 71
tall — dá ndeezé, 109
Taos — Dawoséeo, 6
tasty — dá łika̧'é, 22
tea — dééh, 118
teacher — má'ółkai'íí, 36
terribly — doo ndaade, 56
thank you — ihéedń, 1
that, it — éí, 54
that's nice — éí nzhǫ́, 44
their — mii-, 11
their (more than two) — daamii-, 11
then — ádą́ą́, 86
there (at there) — ą́'ee, ndé'ee, 1, 2
there (to there) — dá'kwéé, 1, 2
they (more than two) — daabíí, 8
they (two) — bíí, 8
thick — diką, 120
think (presume) — át'é nsjį, 101
think about it — ma ííníínaskees, 97
thirsty — bá she'yiiłhį́į́h, 33
this — díí, 3, 4
this one — díí'íí, 52
this particular hat — díí ch'ałíí, 44
this particular road — díí ííkiníí, 54

throat — shiizoł, 51
thunder — idiiníí, 77
Thursday — Ich'énedzoo, 118
time passed — gózhiizh, 80
time passes — gózhísh, 80
tire — bííł miikee, 44
tired — nee nétdeh, 24
tiswin — kółbáíí, 7, 8
to her — miich'į, 74
to me — shiich'į, 74
to my home — shiigha̧'yé, 1, 9
to the east — sháha'áí'yéo, 39
to the mountains — dziłyé, 39
to the north — náakosii'yéo, 39
to the south — shádii'áí'yéo, 39
to the west — shá'ii'áí'yéo, 39
to town, to the store — kįį'yé, 9
to work, to the job — na'iisii'yé, 86
to you — nch'į, 74
today — díijíí, 17
tomatoes — domáadii, 118
tomorrow — yiskáo, 1, 2
too — gó, 56
tooth — shiiwoo, 51
tough — dá diits'idé, 57, 120
town — kįį, 9
tree — chish, 60
true — dá aaníí, 19
try — doo ńdaadégo ásh'íí, 60
Tuesday — Máałdis, 118
turkey — kajee, 119
turtle — ts'óskeeł, 119
twisted — iłk'énasgis, 120

U

uncle — shiida̧'ą́ą́, 119
under it — miiyaayé, 58, 59
understand — diists'e, 3, 4
unreliable — doo ma ch'óolíí da, 72
upon — dah, 90
up there — dágich'į, 58
Ute — Yóda, 6

Ute reservation — Yóda miikéyaa, 27

V

vegetables— neest'áan, 118
visit — ma nshéí, 81, 82

W

wagon — bąąs, 36
wait for it — mííká sézįí, 86
wait — íłtsé, 32
walk about — naashá, 2
walked about — naashá ńtéé, 74
want — hásht'įí, 1, 2
warm — goosdo, 73
warm — sido, 28
warm — dá shił goosdo, 49
wash up — ká'ádiisgis, 86
washed — kanáségis, 105
wash (something) — kanásgis, 105
water — kóh, 12
watermelon — chandíiya, 118
we (more than two) — danahíí, 8
we (two) — nahíí, 8
weak — doo naałwo da, 110
weave — hishtł'ół, 13
Wednesday — Ich'énádzoł, 118
well (adverb) — nzhǫ́go, 25
went — naséyá, 30
west — shá'ii'áí, 39
what about him, her — éíshą, 58
what happened — hat'é ádzaa, 42
what — iiyá', 86
what — iyáná', 6
what else — iyáná' gó, 52
wheat — tł'onaadá', 120
when (future time) — ha'go, 1, 9
when (past time) — ha'dą́, 36
where (at where) — ha'yé, ha'yénąą, 39
where from — ha'shį́įnąą, 20
where to (also *at where*) — ha'yé,
   ha'yénąą, 1, 2
which one — ha'díishą, 52

white — łigai, 62
White Man — Mągáanii, 2
who, whom — ha'ń, 39
why — iyáná'ííká, 98
wife — shii'á, shii'iisdzáníí, 119
willow — k'ai', 119
win — dagoozo, 88
windy — ńyoł, 77
winter — hai, 1, 2
wish — hásht'įí, 1, 2
with me — shił, 2
with you — nił (nł), 2
with, by means of — mee, yee, 34, 35
wolf — ba'iitso, 119
woman — isdzáníí, 110
won — dagóózo, 88
woodpecker — chishkałdéé, 119
work — na'iisii, 12
worked — na'sézii, 12
worried — mą shíínii, 97
wove — sétł'oł, 13
woven — histł'ół, 120
write — ik'e'ishchíí, 93
wrote — ik'e'shéłchį́í, 93

Y

year — hai, 98
years — meeshį́í, 69
yellow — łitso, 62
yes — aoo, 1
yesterday — adádą́, 39
you (more than two) — danahíí, 8
you (singular) — díí, 8
you (two) — nahíí, 8
younger brother — shiishdázha, 119
younger sister — shiishdázha, 119
your (more than two) — danahii-, 11
your (singular) — n-, 11
your (two) — nahii-, 11
your friend — nch'ooníí, 17
yucca — ich'ą́ą́wosh, 119

www.ingramcontent.com/pod-product-compliance
Lightning Source LLC
Chambersburg PA
CBHW080958020726
47505CB00009B/2253